HORMONE PIRATES OF XENOBIA

and

DREAM STUDS OF KAMA LOKA

HORMONE PIRATES OF XENOBIA

and

DREAM STUDS OF KAMA LOKA

TWO NOVELLAS BY ERNEST POSEY

ALYSON PUBLICATIONS
LOS ANGELES

Manufactured in the United States of America.
Printed on acid-free paper.

This trade paperback original is published by Alyson Publications Inc.,
P.O. Box 4371, Los Angeles, California 90078.
Distribution in the United Kingdom by Turnaround Publisher Services Ltd.,
27 Horsell Road, London N5 1XL, England.

First edition: September 1996

5 4 3 2 1

ISBN 1-55583-385-3

Hormone Pirates of Xenobia

DAY ONE

A gruff voice crackled over my headphones: "Identify yourself!" It came over the universal band, where I hadn't heard anything in days. There wasn't supposed to be anyone in this sector of the asteroid belt, and yet here was a voice, speaking in English!

"Identify yourself," the voice repeated, "or I'll blow your ass to smithereens."

I opened the universal band transmitter. "Survey Scout A247, World Syndicate Council. Who are you?"

"Never mind who I am, shithead!" the staticky voice replied. "You're under detention for violating the cubic sector of planetoid Xenobia. Set automatic. We're towing you in, so just sit tight. And don't try any funny stuff!"

Whoever this person was, he sounded like he meant business, so I set up on automatic and waited. I didn't want to take any chances with an unknown assailant, especially with a very expensive new survey craft at stake, to say nothing of my own life and limb.

I looked through the viewport for a likely source of the unknown voice. The nearest visible object from which it could have come was a large rocky planetoid dead ahead, completely barren, black, and covered with pockmarks and craters from meteor collisions.

My suspicions were confirmed after a few moments when a slight jolt informed me that a gravbeam had grabbed my scout ship and was pulling it toward the pocked black spheroid. Soon I saw a rough circular opening appear in one of the larger craters. My spacecraft was drawn into this orifice by the gravbeam, and I found myself in a dimly lit docking bay. There was a mild thump as the ship touched the polished black floor, a metallic clang and the hiss of air as the space repressurized, and then the lights brightened.

I unbuckled my harness, opened the hatch, and stepped out into the unknown: the interior of Xenobia!

No sooner had my feet touched the shiny black floor of the docking bay than a large portal opened in the interior wall, and out emerged four flying robots, looking like a small flock of angels. They were covered with a soft pink plastoid skin, each with a pair of wings spanning about half a meter and a pair of small arms ending in three-fingered hands. Their quasihuman faces resembled those of a cartoon animal. They hovered around me, prodding me toward the door.

Guarded by the levitating robots, I walked into a long corridor and passed numerous doors marked with numbers or strange symbols. Presently the robots made me to stop before a door marked z. The door slid open with a pneumatic hiss.

I entered to find myself facing a giant of a man standing behind a steel desk. He stood at least two meters tall and was built like a work robot, with huge arms, legs, and shoulders, all covered in a silvery metallic body armor. His hair was oily, black, and curly, as was his wiry beard. A gold earring pierced one ear, and his left eye was covered by a black patch.

"So you're the intruder on the sovereign space of Xenobia!" his deep, gravelly voice boomed. "Who are you, and what are you doing in this sector?"

I was impressed and shaken, in spite of my attempt to appear casual. "I'm Antony Stout," I replied. "I'm on an asteroid survey mission for the World Syndicate Council. Who are you?"

"I am Zschado, Magnate of Xenobia," he answered sternly. "In other words, I'm the boss. Your appearance in the sovereign space of Xenobia is unexpected, to say the least."

"No harm intended, Mr. Zschado. I can assure you, I had no idea there were any human outposts in this area. I wasn't even supposed to be surveying near here. Why don't you just let me get on with my work, and we'll just forget the whole thing."

"Har, har, har!" He gave several large belly laughs, and then suddenly turned serious. He sat down behind the desk in a large pneumochair and stared me up and down.

"I'm afraid that it's not that simple," he began. "We can't take any chances that the Council would find out about our operation." He paused for a few moments in thought, a faint smile playing on his lips. "Although I cannot allow you to leave freely, there is perhaps another way of resolving this unfortunate and untimely situation." He paused. "Take off your clothes," he ordered.

"But...why...?" I stammered.

"Cut the crap," he barked. "Strip!"

I pulled off my flight harness, then my pressure suit. I hesitated. "All of it!" he said.

I stripped off my undergear and let it drop to the floor. I was completely naked. He examined my body in clinical fashion, eyeing me from head to toe, particularly my crotch.

He smiled. "How often do you jerk off?" he asked, looking at my prick. "It must get pretty lonely on a survey, being alone for weeks at a time."

"I...I don't know," I said haltingly. "Maybe once or twice a week."

"Do you come a lot?" he asked.

I was startled by the strange turn that this interrogation was beginning to take. "I never thought about it. A normal load, I guess." My prick was beginning to stiffen just thinking about getting my rocks off. I hadn't beaten my meat for several days. I didn't dare look down, but I could feel my nuts tingling and my cock lifting up slightly, starting to swell. I was embarrassed to be getting a hard-on in front of a perfect stranger.

Zschado seemed amused at my discomfort. "I need a demonstration," he said, staring at my thickening tool. "Start jerking so I can check it out."

Hesitatingly I began to stroke my hardening prick. I was horny enough so that I soon overcame my initial embarrassment. I slid my right hand lightly up and down the length of it, stopping at the tip to caress and knead the head, then moving slowly back down the shaft to its hairy base. Zschado watched me intently. After several minutes of this teasingly slow massage, my dick had reached its full erection and stood pointing to the ceiling, engorged and throbbing.

"OK, Mr Stout, that'll be enough," Zschado said. "Take your hands away from your penis and clasp them behind your back." He opened a drawer in the desk and removed a pair of stainless-steel measuring calipers. "Come over here," he ordered.

I approached the desk. Zschado reached forward and grasped my testicles with one muscular hand and with the other slipped the calipers around my left nut. He entered a measurement on a keypad on the desktop, then repeated the same operation with my right nut.

"Hmm, pretty good," he murmured under his breath. "Eighty-three and eighty-seven millimeters."

Then he extended the calipers, setting one point at the base and the other at the tip of my throbbing cock. He entered a figure on the keypad. "Two hundred thirty-three millimeters. Excellent!"

Zschado replaced the calipers in the drawer and leaned back in the pneumochair. He smiled as he surveyed my excited sex tool. "There's one more measurement to be taken."

He pushed a button on the desktop. The door slid open, and two of the pink robots levitated into the room. They hovered over the desk.

"Keep your hands clasped behind your back, Mr. Stout," Zschado instructed. "This won't hurt a bit. The Guardian Angel robots are very efficient, I can assure you. Let me introduce you." He indicated the one on the left. "This is Baker. The other is Charlie."

He drew a clear cylindrical plastoid vial from within the desk and handed it to Charlie, who grasped it with one of its small three-fingered hands. "We will proceed to perform a standard manual extraction on this subject," he commanded. "Stimulation Level 3."

The Guardian Angels homed in on my genitalia. Charlie encircled my scrotum with one pseudohand and held the plastic cylinder near the tip of my erect penis with the other. Baker grasped the swollen shaft of my prick with one hand while closing the other around the head. Their hands began to vibrate mechanically, excitingly, moving up and down in a steady rhythm. The pink plastoid "skin" was warm and squishy. Baker and Charlie hummed and whirred in time to their up-and-down bobbing movements. Time seemed to stand still while I was undergoing this exquisite stimulation. I gazed down at the otherworldly spectacle of these two floating devices, pink and soft, pulling and kneading my engorged rod and swollen nuts. The vibrations were unendurably maddening. This slow and unnerving stimulation continued for some minutes, during which Zschado leered at the spectacle from behind his desk.

I soon seemed to be almost on the brink of ejaculation, and yet I could not shoot. The robots' hands continued to massage my cock and balls. "Please..." I moaned. "Please, Mr. Zschado, let me shoot my load—or make them stop."

"*I'll* decide when you will ejaculate!" he retorted.

"I don't know how much more of this I can take!"

"Now, now, Mr. Stout, don't be a sissy. A big man such as yourself should be able to withstand a level of stimulation far in excess of that which you are now undergoing. I am about to make you an important offer, one that could change your life. Everything depends on your reaction to this simple test that you are now experiencing. Would you perhaps like to proceed to Stimulation Level 4?"

A moan escaped my lips from the unendurable pleasure that Baker and Charlie were inflicting on my helpless organs. They were tireless, relentless, and very strong. I didn't know how much more I could stand, but I had to answer the challenge Zschado had posed. I found myself mouthing the words "OK, proceed to Stimulation Level 4."

"Baker, Charlie: Stimulation Level 4!" Zschado ordered. "Keep your hands behind your back, Mr Stout. The Angels don't like to be interfered with while they are at work."

He pressed a button on the desk console and called, "Delta, come in!" The two Angels were joined by a third, which entered the room from the corridor. Newcomer Angel Delta stationed itself behind me and began to probe my anus with one of its fingers, twisting and turning until it found my bare prostate. Baker and Charlie continued to pound my sex meat.

"No," I gasped, my breath coming in deep, heaving gulps.

"Oh, yes, Mr. Stout." said Zschado. "You see, the Angels have minute sensors under all parts of their pseudoskin that enable them to both send and receive electrical signals. They are able to sense, by galvanic skin responses, when you are about to achieve orgasm. But they can also, by the use of certain programmable electroneural outputs, delay or indefinitely postpone your orgasm. You may never achieve orgasm unless it is by my order!"

Pulling...twisting...kneading...the dynamic mechanical arms of Charlie worked on my overloaded testicles. Delta's long finger extended into my rectum, pushing rhythmically at my burning prostate, and each time it touched, it emitted a sparklike electrical current, which then raced into my nuts. My knees were getting weak, near to collapsing. Still, I couldn't take my eyes off those little pink fleshy hands working on my cock and balls.

I looked up imploringly at Zschado. A gigantic bulge in the links of the body armor at his crotch revealed the extent of his cruel involvement in this excruciating sport. "Had enough, Mr. Stout?" he asked, a sardonic smile on his full red lips. "How about just a few minutes of stimulation at Level 5 before we call it a day?" He began to massage the swelling between his legs casually with his left hand. "Baker, Charlie, Delta!" he barked. "Stimulation Level 5!"

Whack! Whack! Whack! Whack! Baker's pounding of my turgid meat seemingly doubled in force. I gasped in agony. My knees collapsed, and I felt as if I were being held up by my dick and by Delta's probing finger up my ass.

How much time had passed? I was held in suspended animation on the brink of orgasm. All I was aware of was the rhythmic pounding, jerking, pounding, jerking of my almost raw dick shaft. The ecstasy of the pleasure-pain was too much to bear.

Finally I heard Zschado's deep, commanding voice. "Mr. Stout!" I focused on his face, where a satisfied smile lingered. He rubbed his huge erect prick through his armor, showing no sign of shame whatsoever. "Time for extraction," he said. "Baker! Charlie! Delta! Extract now!"

Charlie clamped the plastic vial tightly over the head of my penis to catch the ejaculate. Baker grabbed the extreme base of my dick and began to squeeze tightly as its hand vibrated the area of the shaft just below the head. The coup de grâce came instantly as Delta applied a forceful electric current through my prostate that raced downward into my engorged testicles.

"Ha!" exclaimed Zschado as we both watched torrents of viscous white sperm flow from the swollen red head of my penis. Spurt after spurt shot into the clear cylinder held in place by Charlie. The electric current to my prostate was timed by Delta's minisensors to maximize semen production. On and on the spumes of frothy come sprayed the sides of the plastic cylinder. Huge spurts: One. Two. Three. I writhed and twitched. Four. Five. The electronic sparks zapped my prostate. Six. Gushing creamy gobs of man juice. My pelvic muscles heaved. Seven. My cock jerked up and down in painful spasms. Eight. "Wow!" Zschado breathed in wonder. Nine. Ten! Eleven! Twelve! On and on it came. Twenty. It was down to a dribble now. Twenty-one. Drip, drip, drop...

The robots released their grip. I fell panting and heaving to my knees. "Holy Jupiter!" I gasped.

"Extraordinary!" exclaimed Zschado. He was looking at the plastic vial full of sperm that Charlie had handed to him. "An excellent extraction. More—much more—than I expected!"

I struggled to my feet. My cock and balls were purple and throbbing like a bass drum. I heard Zschado's voice as if from a great distance, saying, "Congratulations, my boy! I'm going to offer you a contract. Baker, Delta—bring Mr. Stout a chair."

The robots levitated into the room with a pneumochair, grasped me under the arms, and flopped me into a seated position. The chair adjusted itself to my weight.

"I know you're wondering what's going on here," he said, gazing at the mass of white cream in the vial he held up to the light. "To put it briefly, here on Xenobia we're in the business of selling sperm." He paused, as if he didn't want to overwhelm me all at once with this peculiar business. "We are selling sperm to aliens. To the Vronks."

I *was* overwhelmed. "Then...then they're real?" I asked him. "There really are aliens? On Earth you hear only rumors—but you've actually seen them?"

"Oh, yes. They are surely real. I've seen them and talked to them. Not a pretty sight, I can tell you. Not pretty at all. On the other hand, they're actually very nice when you get to know them, almost like getting to know a child or an animal.

"Well, anyway," Zschado continued, "when they first made contact, it was with certain persons on the Mars colony at Nuevahavana. It seems the main thing they're interested in from the human race is large quantities of our sperm. Naturally, where there's a demand, someone will show up to produce a supply. That's where I come in. I run the sperm extractors of Xenobia. It's not exactly legal, but then, it's not exactly illegal either. Our best guarantee of having no trouble is for the Council and its agents to know nothing at all about our operation. That's why we can't just turn you loose."

I couldn't believe my ears at the bizarre story Zschado was telling me. My incredulity must have been written all over my face, because he said, "It's all true. Why would I lie at this point?

"I want to offer you a proposition," he added. "A contract, actually. Sign up for three months on the sperm extractors. You simply agree to give us all of your sperm production for the next three months. Your salary for that short period will be 350 million universal credits. You can leave after that time, with no questions asked. You see, by then you'll be an accomplice, so you'll be highly unlikely to blab to the authorities about our operations here on Xenobia.

"You'll be on the extractor one day out of three—in other words, every third day—with two days to rest and recover,"

Zschado went on. "So you get all that money for only about thirty days of actual 'work.' There are other benefits as well. What do you say?"

I was amazed. "That's about five years' regular salary for a survey scout," I said. "But what about the sperm you just extracted against my will? Do I get paid for that? And will the other extractions be this, shall I say, forceful?"

"Good questions, Mr. Stout. The sperm in this vial that I hold in my hand we shall consider payment of the fine you owe for violating the cubic space of Xenobia.

"The subsequent extractions will be done on a special device designed specifically for that purpose," he continued. "In short, it is a totally different experience from the rather, I admit, unnerving test you have just endured so well and passed with flying colors."

He looked at the large quantity of sperm in the vial. "You will be a very good producer," he said. "The Vronks pay very well, Mr. Stout, and so we pass a handsome profit on to our spermstuds. Even though we are pirates here on Xenobia, we have a code of ethics. This is a business first and foremost. So rest assured that at the end of your contract, you'll be paid promptly in gold bullion, which can't be traced. So what do you say, Mr. Stout? Is it a deal?"

I didn't have to think very long because I didn't have much choice. "OK," I said, and I signed the document he placed on the desk a few moments later. I didn't even bother to read it. What would have been the use? How could I argue with this sperm pirate, who had me literally by the balls?

"Baker will show you to your room, which will be on Level 6," Zschado informed me. "Your spermstud number is 677. We don't use names here. You'll start on the extractor tomorrow morning at 0800 hours, when you will report to Room 666. Come see me here in this office if you have any problems, questions, or difficulties of any kind."

My knees were still shaky when I stood up. Zschado took a black tunic from a cabinet. It was made of soft veloid and had a white number on the back and on the left front: 677. I slipped it on. It reached just to my knees and fastened down the front with magloops. He gave me a pair of soft black veloid boots to wear.

"Enjoy your stint on Xenobia!" he called as Baker nudged me out the door and into the corridor.

Zschado's office was on Level 1. Guardian Angel Baker took me on a pneumolift down to Level 6. The complex on Xenobia was essentially a cylindrical building carved into the interior of the planetoid. Any of the circular corridors would eventually lead back to its starting point. Each corridor had two pneumolifts that went up or down to the other levels. The hallways were lined with doors and illuminated with soft, dim lights. Pink robot angels occasionally hurried by, darting and floating to their unknown errands.

We arrived at a door marked 677, matching my spermstud number. The door slid open to reveal a small room with a bed, a table, two small pneumochairs, and a cabinet against the back wall. Hovering in the center of the room was a robot with the number 677 stenciled on its belly. My personal Guardian Angel! Was it my valet or my jailer?

A small diagram lay on the table. It showed the plan of the interior of Xenobia. Each level was laid out pretty much the same, except that large areas were not marked. Unknown territory. But there were familiar things as well, including a restaurant on each level. MEALS AT ALL HOURS, the caption read. I decided to find the restaurant for Level 6. I was starving after my bizarre masturbatory workout. It was easy to find—just down the corridor from my cubicle.

Double doors marked RESTAURANT slid open to reveal a large room holding about two dozen round tables with matching pneumochairs. A number of men in black tunics like mine were eating, drinking, or talking in subdued voices. Some were in groups, some alone. Everyone looked up and gave me the once-over when I entered the room, then quickly returned to what they were doing. Several angels darted about carrying trays of food and drink.

I was wondering what to do next when a tall silver-haired Lunarian approached. He smiled. "You're new," he said. "I can always tell. Join me at my table, won't you?" His tunic indicated that he was spermstud number 660. As we sat, he waved for an Angel waiter.

"What's your pleasure?" he asked.

"What's on the menu?" I queried.

"Anything you want. Everything is synthesized, so they can make anything you ask for. Some things are better than others. Try the cheese omelette. It's almost natural-tasting." I nodded. He addressed the Angel waiter. "And bring two coffees also." The angel rushed off. He turned back to me. "So how long have you been in Xenobia?" he asked.

"Just a few hours," I answered. "My first extractor session is tomorrow at 0800 hours. I don't know what to expect. Zschado wasn't very explicit."

"Don't worry, it's not so bad. I'm used to it. This is my third thirty-day contract, and I'm still alive, as you can see." He looked at me sympathetically. "Did Zschado set his personal Guardian Angels on you?"

"He sure did," I answered, glancing down at my crotch, where my dick still throbbed from its mauling. "Does he do that to everybody who comes to Xenobia?"

"Usually, I guess. He did it to me the first time I was here. I suppose it's really meant to be a test of your productive capabilities. But the extractor machines are quite different—not so, shall we say, brutal."

I looked him over. Aside from the extremely white skin, which was common to all Lunarians, he seemed to be in excellent health. His tunic was pulled tight over a set of broad shoulders, and his legs, visible from below the lower hem, were thick and well-muscled. His pale, silvery hair gleamed in the soft light of the restaurant.

"Is it true what Zschado told me about the aliens—the Vronks?" I asked him. "Do they really want human sperm? What do they use it for?"

"It's true, as far as I know," he replied. "Some people say that the aliens get their jollies by ingesting it, because they have no sexuality of their own. Others say they're using it for incomprehensible biochemical experiments. Whatever the case, they pay through the nose for it. The Vronks know how to transmute metals, so they pay for it in pure gold. No one knows how much, except maybe Zschado himself. But it's a lot—many, many times over what the spermstuds get paid. Maybe fifty, maybe a hundred times more."

The Angel arrived with a tray. The omelette it placed on the table looked real. The coffee smelled OK. "What are the benefits Zschado mentioned that aren't listed in the contract?" I asked through a mouthful of food.

"Well, the most obvious is the phenomenon of permanent genital enlargement, which happens gradually and progressively during your stints on the extractors. It probably also has a lot to do with the megahormones they feed us."

I stopped chewing and gulped. "You mean...?"

"Yes," he replied. "Everything on Xenobia is laced with synthetic hormones, including your omelette and even the coffee we're drinking. You can see why, if you think a bit. The bottom line here is sperm production, so the directors do everything within the range of human know-how to increase it to the max. They put us spermstuds on the extractors once every three days because they've discovered that three days is the testicular recovery time for the best production by volume."

"How did you get here?" I asked.

"I volunteered. I heard about Xenobia in Lunacolony, where I was born. When I found out what they pay, it made up my mind real fast. I'm on my third contract, and I intend to do one more, for a total of a year. I'll be a rich man when I return to Luna. With the right investments I can retire at twenty-eight and never have to work again."

"What do you do with your days off?" I asked.

"That's the hardest part," he answered. "The hormones keep you loaded with energy. You don't have to exercise because the hormones keep your muscles toned. Myself, I read or watch discs or shoot the shit with the other spermstuds. Some guys have sex with each other, but that's forbidden here. You have to sneak around to do it. That's why the Guardian Angel is in your room—to stop you from any unauthorized release of sperm, either by yourself or with someone else. The studs who go for that sort of thing have to avoid the Guardian Angels. Zschado wants all of the sperm produced on Xenobia for himself, to sell to the Vronks. None must be wasted for recreational purposes."

"Well, I'm not into that kind of sex," I stated. "I don't have anything against men who do, but it's just never been my thing." I chewed the last of my omelette and took the last swallow of hormoned coffee.

"I know how you feel about that kind of sexual activity," he said. "I've never gone in for it either. As a matter of fact, I have a mate and two offspring back on Luna."

He looked at the chronometer over the door. "You'd better be getting some sleep if you're going to get juiced tomorrow at 0800. I'll walk with you back to your cube."

His referring to being on the extractor device as "getting juiced" made me realize that this whole strange experience might become commonplace after a while. As we entered the corridor, I asked, "What's it like getting juiced—I mean, being on the extractor?"

"Everyone here refers to it as getting juiced, and it's different for everybody, even though the actual process is the same," he explained. "People react differently. Some say it's nothing, that they're indifferent to it. Others say they look forward to it and can't wait for their two holidays to be over so they can get back on the juicer. Me, I happen to like it, which is why I've signed up for three contract periods, aside from the money. It's a very different experience from getting mauled by Zschado's Angels. But just wait until tomorrow morning, and you'll see for yourself."

He paused in front of a door marked URINAL. He looked around. There was no one in the corridor. "Quick, come in here," he whispered. "I want to show you what I was talking about."

The room was empty except for a sloping stainless-steel depression in the center of the floor shaped like a big funnel about two meters in diameter; around this urine-disposal funnel was a tubular steel railing at waist height to prevent anyone from sliding in while he pissed. My companion stepped up to the railing. He waited until I stood beside him, and then he pulled open the magloops on his veloid tunic to reveal an enormous white mule dick with heavy-hanging testicles to match.

"Great Neptune!" I gasped in awe. He started to take a leak, and I could compare his piss stream only to that of a stallion in a parade. He slapped this donkey meat several times against his thigh to shake off the last drops. He paused before fastening his tunic so that I could admire his magnificent tool.

"Seen enough?" he asked, smiling at my amazement. "This is the result of seventy-four sessions on the juicer—and the megahormones, of course. One thing you'll do is start to count the juicing sessions. Tomorrow is my seventy-fifth." He looked down to admire his own massive manhood. It hung halfway down to his knees. He gave it one last meaty slap. "Pretty amazing, huh?"

I stared in astonishment as he refastened the magloops of his tunic. "And I expect to gain a few more centimeters by the time I finish my fourth contract," he said as we continued down the corridor.

We stopped in front of my door, number 677. "Here's your cube," he said. "By the way, my name's Bron. What's yours?"

"I thought we weren't supposed to use names here."

"Oh, nobody listens to that shit," he replied. "What are they going to do if you disobey—fire your ass? What's your name?"

"I'm Antony."

"Well, sleep soundly, Antony." He clapped his big hand on my shoulder and disappeared down the long, curving hallway. I threw myself on my bunk and fell almost instantly into a deep, uninterrupted sleep.

DAY TWO

All too soon, it seemed, my Guardian Angel was prodding me awake. A voice came over the overhead speaker in the ceiling. "Extractor shift 0800! Extractor shift 0800!"

I hurried out into the corridor. Unlike the previous night, there were many men hurrying about, all wearing the same identical black tunic and boots. I walked quickly to door number 666. It slid open with a hiss.

A tall, heavyset man in a white smock was waiting for me. He wore gold-rimmed spectacles and sported a shock of flaming red hair and a red mustache and goatee. He looked up as I entered the room.

"Good morning, Spermstud 677," he exclaimed, beaming at me. "Let me introduce myself. I'm Dr. Sax." He shook my hand warmly and indicated the room with a wave of his arm. "To lessen the stress and unfamiliarity of the situation, your first day on the extractor will be in this private cubicle. After today you will be in a larger extractor room with twenty other spermstuds. However, you'll have a better idea of what's going on after we get started. So if you don't mind, we'll begin right away."

He indicated a black plastoid table in the center of the room. "Please be kind enough to remove your tunic and footwear and lie faceup on the table."

I did as he instructed. The black plastoid felt squishy and faintly warm. Dr. Sax immediately began placing soft restraints around my ankles, thighs, waist, chest, and neck.

"Don't be alarmed," he said. "These are simply meant to keep you from injuring yourself during the course of the extraction. I'll explain everything to you as we go along so you'll understand what's happening."

He began to knead my penis with his big, strong hands, and soon it started to harden perceptibly.

"I need to have your penis at full erection before attaching the extractor unit," he explained. After a few more minutes of his expert massaging, my cock was fully erect—hard as a rock and pointing straight up.

"Very good," said Dr. Sax. "You respond extremely well. By the way, Zschado told me that your sperm production is most impressive. I'm looking forward to seeing you prove to be one of our finest spermstuds."

From the side of the room he wheeled a large machine clad in stainless steel supporting an overhead boom from which were dangling numerous tubes, cables, and electrodes. He began to lubricate my hard cock with slimy pale blue jelly. He slid his hands up and down my cock until the entire shaft and head were covered with the gel.

"Erectogel is specially formulated to insure proper mechanical and electrical contact with the extractor unit," he explained as he massaged my rock-hard dick with the slimy substance.

The blue gel seemed to contain some strange yet stimulating chemical because as Dr. Sax's hands slid up and down, my cock began to throb and tingle in an unfamiliar way.

When my prick was thoroughly coated with the gel, he pulled down from the overhead unit a large clear plastoid tube with a thick black ring at the base. He slid this tube over my throbbing, tingling dick and began to press buttons on the machine. The black ring contracted until it had grabbed the base of my erect cock firmly.

"The Erectogel combined with the compression ring at the base of your penis ensures that you will maintain full erection for the entire eight hours of the extraction," Dr. Sax said.

"Eight hours!" I exclaimed.

"Yes," he answered. "Actually, seven hours and fifty minutes. We have a ten-minute break between extractor shifts. But I assure you that the time will pass very quickly. In fact, some people think it's too short." He smiled at me mischievously. The extractor tube with its compression ring tightened again on the base of my already steel-hard penis.

"Now, don't be alarmed at the next step, but in a few moments you will feel something entering the urethra. It is the heart of the extraction process."

Within moments I felt a small, slimy probe slide into the opening of my rigid cock, which was now held firmly inside the extractor tube. A warm, tingling sensation began at the glans, and as the object slid farther and farther inside my penis, the prickling warmth slowly extended downward until it had reached the base of my dick.

"You see, the internal sperm duct is now extended into the entire length of your penis," explained Dr. Sax. "This guarantees that we will achieve maximum sperm production and collection." He smiled down at me benevolently. "Just a few more simple attachments, and we will be ready to begin."

He drew down two electrodes from the overhead boom and attached them lightly, one to each of my testicles. Then from the base of the table he pulled a long, springy cable that ended in a plastoid ring. This he attached around my scrotum so that the cable stretched my testicles downward with a strong pressure, pulling them away from my groin and toward my feet.

"These are to provide testicular stimulation and monitoring," he said. "You see, we don't allow orgasm to occur during extraction. Your biochemical state will be one in which you will be held close to orgasm for the full seven hours and fifty minutes but never allowed to cross that orgasmic barrier. We have discovered that once the subject achieves orgasm, the body's hormone-production systems tend to shut down for a few hours, and this, of course, is not desirable for our purposes."

Next, a long metal rod with a bright stainless-steel sphere at the tip was lubricated with the blue Erectogel and deftly inserted by Dr. Sax's strong fingers into my anus. He shoved it in about fifteen centimeters, until the ball-like tip was resting firmly against my prostate gland.

"This is to provide prostatic stimulation. It is monitored by the computer within the extraction unit. At certain necessary intervals, indicated by the extractor's electronic sensors, a small electrical charge will be passed into the prostate to stimulate further sperm production."

I had as yet felt no sensations from the extractor other than the tingling from the Erectogel inside and outside my erect dick and a similar prickling from the rod inside my anus.

"Just one more thing, and we'll be ready to start," he said.

From beneath the table he produced a large helmetlike device, which he slipped over my head. It fit snugly, with the top pressing lightly against my temples.

"This is the neurotransmitter," he explained. "It does many things, but what you will be chiefly concerned with is that it will eliminate any possibility of boredom during your stint on the extractor."

He pulled down a rubberoid mouthpiece with a tube leading into it. It fit snugly over my upper teeth. The tube began to drip a fruit-flavored elixir into my mouth that trickled slowly down my throat. I had never tasted anything like it before.

"These are megahormone drops. They not only help to maximize sperm production but also provide certain pleasant psychological side effects, which you are sure to notice."

He stepped back and looked up and down at my naked body, strapped to the table. I was completely immobilized, helpless.

"Now, let's see if we're ready," Dr. Sax said. "Restraints in place. Extractor tube and internal sperm duct in place. Testicular cable and electrodes in place. Prostatic monitor and stimulator in place. Megahormone drip mouthpiece in place. Neurotransmitter helmet in place. Checklist complete!"

He looked down into my eyes. "You won't be able to see anything in the room until it's time for you to leave the table at 1550 hours. So I'll say good-bye now, and I'll see you then."

He flipped down the face mask of the helmet so that all I could see was a field of translucent white. I could sense the hormone drops trickling down from the tube in my mouth, the sweet, fruity taste bathing the back of my tongue and throat.

The white visor screen began to glow with a faint color, first a deep red, shading into orange, and then very slowly into yellow, green, and blue. Tiny flashing lights began to appear on the screen, making intricate geometric patterns.

It seemed like a long time before I was aware of any new sensations in my rock-hard dick, but gradually I realized that the extractor was at work. Almost imperceptibly, over a period of many minutes, I began to sense that the extractor tube was moving very slightly with a faint up-and-down motion—an almost throbbing movement. At the same time, it seemed to be contracting and expanding, as if it were squeezing my dick. The rubberoid base, I could tell now, was moving up and down very slightly, perhaps only one or two centimeters, and very slowly. I could also now feel a definite movement in the cable that was stretching my testicles. It too was moving back and forth only a few centimeters at a time, pulling my balls and then releasing. The feeling of warmth increased gradually as the extractor tube heated up. The metal electrode nestling up against my prostate gland began to tingle faintly and seemed almost hot. My cock felt harder than I had ever remembered in my life. The inside of my tormented prick pushed outward against the skin as if trying to burst through. Hot blood rushed through the distended veins, and the head throbbed rhythmically.

After I endured many more minutes of this excruciating, tingling, torturous pleasure, it seemed as if the activity in the extractor tube was increasing. The seminal-duct tube that filled my urethra from top to base seemed to be pulsating, giving rise to strange, unbearable tickling sensations that ran up and down the entire inside length of my cock. It was as if I were being jerked off from the inside out. Then the electrodes attached to my testicles began to tingle, and a current seemed to run back and forth from one ball to the other, setting my gonads aflame. The extractor tube got hotter and hotter, suffusing the entire length of my engorged dick with heat.

And then it seemed as if the tube were vibrating very slightly in addition to its up-and-down motion. All of these sensations at once seemed to be leading me inexorably, gently, and mercilessly toward an intense climax.

The colored patterns on the screen in front of my eyes danced and pulsated, and I began to think that I could hear a faint sound. It sounded like a deep moaning that was at a great distance but that gradually began to come closer. Was the sound made by a machine or by an animal? It repeated over and over: "Uhhhmmm...uhhhmmm...uhhhmmm..."

It was the sound of something struggling in the throes of intense orgasmic thrills. The sound seemed to come closer and then fade. Then it became louder and then faded again.

I gradually became aware that all of these strange sensations—the lights dancing in front of my eyes, the repeated deep moaning sounds, the heat and tingling against my prostate, the flashes of energy darting back and forth between my testicles, the wriggling and pulsing of the sperm duct inside my urethra, the heat suffusing the shaft of my throbbing dick, the back-and-forth motions of the cable pulling my testicles, the vibrating column of my cock—seemed to be coming in perfectly timed waves. I knew I was on the brink of an intense orgasm—and yet it wouldn't occur. But now hot trickles of what seemed like molten lava began to run up from my testicles and into the the sperm-collecting probe. The moaning increased. It was as if I were experiencing an extremely prolonged preorgasm.

I gave myself over to the power of the machine. I was helpless before its inexorable electronic will. I had become its unwitting slave, or, perhaps, even more accurately, I had become a part of the machine itself, a small particle of flesh, merely an adjunct to its steely purpose.

I watched the flashes of kaleidoscopic colored lights dancing before my eyes on the visor screen and felt the wonders of the surging sensations running through my entire body. Wave after wave of intense and unalterable pleasure surged from my groin, through my chest, into my head, and then back. It was as if I were on a small raft tossing on the waves of a warm tropical sea. The waves passed back and forth, back and forth, from my groin to my stomach to my chest to my neck to the top of my head and then down again. I could feel my body writhing like a snake, pulling and straining against the straps that held me to the table. My spine alternately flexed up and down like the waves of the ocean on which I floated.

In time to these waves of muscular contractions and releases, the torrid stream of hot lava surged out of my distended gonads and moved slowly upward into the sperm-collection probe within my urethra, burning as it flowed. My head throbbed with the repeated moaning. "Uhhhmmm...uhhhmmm...uhhhmmm..."

The waves gradually became softer and quieter. The screen darkened, and stars came out overhead. I was floating now on my raft on the warm tropical sea. I was lying completely calmly, looking up at the stars against the black backdrop of infinity.

The view screen flipped up. "Well, how was your first day on the extractor?" Dr. Sax said, smiling down at me.

"What?" I exclaimed. "Is it over already? Eight hours?"

"Seven hours and fifty minutes, to be exact. Everyone has that experience the first time—I mean, that compression of time. It's something you'll get used to."

He pried open my left eyelid and then my right, peering into my pupils. "Good, good," he said. "No sign of any undue stress. Let me get you disengaged from the machine, then I can answer any more questions you may have."

He slid the helmet off my head, then released the cable from my testicles and removed the electrodes. He next slid the prostate probe from my anus, wiping it clean before dropping it into a sterilizer. He pressed a few buttons on the extractor console, and the tube that had held my rigid cock all day slid off and upward with a slurping sound. My penis was still rock-hard, purple, and engorged with blood. And—amazingly—it looked somewhat larger than before.

Although disengaged from the machine, I was still strapped to the table. Dr. Sax began to poke at my rigid penis with his finger. "Hmm," he said. "Good. Still a firm erection. I must compliment you, Spermstud 677. Your endurance is excellent."

He wiped off my dick with a clean towel that he then dropped into the disposal chute. He released the straps on my neck, chest, thighs, and ankles, putting his beefy hand behind my neck and helping me into a sitting position on the table.

"How do you feel?" he asked.

"I feel wonderful," I said brightly. "I feel terrific! And I'm very hungry."

"Well, good," Dr. Sax replied. "It looks like you had a good reaction to your first day."

He was looking at one of the digital readouts on the machine.

"This is amazing!" he breathed. "Your sperm production has been the largest recorded in the entire history of Xenobia. Because our techniques are so advanced, this is a wonderful surprise. It shows how science can triumph over nature, does it not? My boy, we expect great things from you. Now, run along. Go to the restaurant and get yourself some food. You need the nourishment, and you need the hormones as well, to keep up your production levels."

He handed me my black tunic and helped me slip it on. I fastened the magloops, but it was plainly evident beneath the soft veloid fabric that my dick was still rock-hard.

With a wave of his hand, Dr. Sax opened the door to the corridor. "We'll expect to see you in Room 606 at 0800 hours two days from now. That's Sevenday, I believe."

"But..." I said, looking down at my erect dick poking through the tunic.

Dr. Sax gave a little laugh. "The shift is over, and you'll see lots of erect penises in the corridor and in the restaurant," he explained. "I'm afraid that after a treatment on the extractor, you will stay that way for at least half an hour, maybe more. You'll get used to it. Everyone else here does. No one will notice."

I walked out into the corridor and headed in the direction of the restaurant. There were dozens of men of all sizes, shapes, and colors walking to and fro, some in a hurry, some walking slowly, some in pairs, some alone. At least half of them had bulges in the front of their tunics betraying large postextraction erections. No one seemed to take notice. I nonchalantly walked along the corridor like everyone else until I came to the restaurant.

As I walked in, I saw Bron seated at the same table where we had had our conversation the previous evening. When he saw me he smiled. He waved his hand, motioning me over. As I sat down across from him, he noticed my erect dick.

"Well, how was your first day on the extractor?" he asked.

I couldn't help smiling as I said, "It was wonderful! I...I...liked it. It was great!"

"Yes," he said, "I enjoy it too. So we have something in common. Now, I suppose you're hungry. Everybody is hungry when they get off the extractors."

"Yes, indeed," I replied. "I'm starving."

Bron waved to a Guardian Angel. "Let me order for you," he said. "Since I've been around here for so long, I know what's good and what's not. Trust me?"

I nodded. "Two sirloin tips with rice, and two lagers," he ordered. The Angel hurried off.

"I was amazed that the time passed so quickly on the extractor," I told him, struggling for words to describe the experience. "It seemed as if I had the helmet on my head for only about fifteen minutes. I seemed to be in a kind of dreamlike state. There were waves...like orgasmic waves...except it wasn't orgasm. I could feel strange things in my penis, hot flashes of...of..."

"Semen," Bron said, finishing my sentence for me. "Yes, you see, they bring you to the point of orgasm with the hormones, with the electrical stimulation, with the pulling and vibrating of your testicles and of your penis. All of this is timed with certain lights and sounds that are generated from within the helmet. They bring you to the point of orgasm and keep you there. And then, stimulated by the hormones, the sperm begins to flow from your testicles into the tube they've inserted in your dick. And it continues to flow, little by little, for eight hours. Pretty clever, isn't it?"

"Sacred Saturn," I said. "You mean the sperm flows continuously the whole time?"

"That's right," said Bron. "It doesn't shoot out, of course, like a normal ejaculation—it flows in a steady kind of drip and gets sucked up by the tube in your urethra, from where it's collected into a reservoir in the extractor machine, where it's kept at a certain temperature. Later it gets sent to Zschado's sperm vault, which, I gather, is in a secret place somewhere inside Xenobia. Its location isn't on any of the diagrams. By the way," he added, "has your prick softened yet?"

I looked down. It had been about ten minutes since I left the extractor room. My dick was still poking up through the black material of my tunic. I looked up at Bron sheepishly. "No," I replied. "It's still hard."

Bron smiled. "There's an easy way to get it to go down." His eyes twinkled. "Just use your hand and give it a good hard slap or two. That usually works."

"Right in here?" I asked.

"Oh, sure!" he replied. "No one pays any attention to that. You see spermstuds slapping their dicks around all the time to get them to go down. I mean, after a day on the extractor, it's a bit uncomfortable to have your dick stay rock-hard for so long."

I looked around the restaurant. "I'll pass on that for right now," I said. "I'll just wait for it to soften."

The Angel waiter arrived with two trays of food and placed them on the table. I couldn't attempt to be polite. I grabbed a fork and started to dig into the food as if I'd been starving for months. My mouth was full when a question occurred to me. I swallowed and asked, "Is it OK to go to the other levels? I noticed that everyone on this level has a 6 as the beginning number on his tunic."

"Oh, sure," said Bron. "It's OK to go anywhere on Xenobia, because the forbidden areas are not accessible anyway. Some people say that the only way into the secret areas is through the door marked Z, which, of course, is Zschado's office. So you're allowed to take the pneumolifts to any of Xenobia's seven levels. But most people don't go to any other level, because they all have the same things: restaurant, private cubicles, shower rooms, urinals, toilets, extractor rooms, etc. Except for Level 1—that's where the recreation facilities are located."

I heard a loud slapping sound. Turning to look at the table to my right, I noticed a spermstud hitting his erect dick. Pow! Pow! Pow! He had taken it out of his tunic and was holding the shaft in his left hand while administering a series of powerful slaps to the top of it with his right. His stiff meat was huge—not as big as Bron's, but almost. He must have been a veteran spermstud, on his second or third contract, to have experienced such genital enlargement. After the fifth strong slap, his dick suddenly subsided in his hand and went limp. He breathed a sigh of relief, laid his dick on the chair, closed his tunic, and resumed eating.

"See?" said Bron. "It works."

"I'll still pass," I said, shoveling another mouthful of rice into my face. "What is there to do on your days off, Bron?"

"There's lots to do," he said. "Why don't you come to my cubicle when you wake up in the morning? You have two days off, and so do I. We're both on pretty much the same extractor shifts. I'll show you some things we can do."

"Good," I said. "I'll see you then."

"When you get back to your cube," Bron told me, "look in the compartment against the back wall. There's an information holodisc you can put into the player inside. It shows you the official story of Xenobia. Of course, it doesn't tell you everything— just what they want you to know, really—but it does have some information in it. If you have any questions, we'll talk about it tomorrow."

After a few more minutes of conversation, we said good night to each other. As we were leaving, a stud at the next table grabbed my arm. It was the same man who had slapped his prick a few minutes before. I looked him over carefully, noting his stocky, muscular physique; his coppery skin; and the fact that he had no body hair whatsoever—not even on his head. I wondered what race he belonged to. His tunic bore the number 678. The cube next to mine…

"Hey, I like newcomers!" he said, smiling. "Especially one as cute as you are. Why don't you come over to my cube later on, and we'll have some fun?"

27

"No thanks," I replied quickly, pulling my arm from his strong grip and hurrying away.

I went back to my cubicle, threw off my tunic, and slipped off my boots. I found the information holodisc and shoved it into the player. I pressed the start button and lay back on the bunk. The image placed itself directly overhead by retinal feedback. The ceiling seemed to dissolve over the bed, and a holographic image formed. I could see Xenobia slowly rotating against the starry blackness of space much as I had seen it from the viewport of my scout ship. Was it only yesterday? It seemed like weeks ago. So much had happened...

"This is Xenobia, the first planetoid in the solar system to be developed and inhabited by humans," the narrator's deep voice began. "Planetoid Xenobia is approximately 2.2 kilometers in diameter, is roughly spherical, and is composed of a homogenous mass of black basalt. It was discovered in the year 103 by the Polish cosmonaut Vishnevski, who named it after his grandmother. The planetoid is unique in that its composition offers superb insulating qualities against solar radiation. The city of Xenobia is carved into the solid core of the planetoid and is a cylindrical construction on seven levels, measuring 200 meters in diameter and 300 meters in height."

At this point a cutaway view of Xenobia appeared, showing very much the same information that was on the map I had studied on the table the previous night.

The narration continued. "Xenobia is equipped with three cold-fusion units, which supply its power in the amount of 3,870 megawatts per solar day. This power is used to keep the entire habitable interior of Xenobia at a constant temperature of twenty-two degrees Celsius and at twenty-five percent relative humidity. The artificial gravity units are located beneath the bottom level of the city and provide a constant gravity roughly equal to that of Earth."

My mind wandered. I thought about my little scout ship, now captive somewhere in the bowels of the planetoid. After a few weeks I would be considered LIS: lost in space. Soon it would be as if I had never existed. But in three months I would leave Xenobia with 350 million credits in gold! I could go anywhere in the solar system, do anything I chose. Start a new life.

I fell asleep as the deep voice droned on and on with facts, figures, and other trivia about Xenobia. In my dreams I saw Xenobia herself, an old Polish grandmother, laughing, her wrinkled face contorted in paroxysms of evil glee, as if she were privy to some cosmic practical joke.

DAY THREE

I knocked on the door of Bron's cubicle. The door slid open. He was lying on the bed, looking at a book. "Good morning, Antony," he said.

"Well," I replied, "there are books on Xenobia!"

"Yes," he answered, "lots of them. Also, lots of holodiscs, learning cartridges for holographic studies, gymnasiums, viewport lounges. Zschado's income from the aliens is so immense that he can afford to equip his domain with every imaginable recreation. He knows that a happy spermstud is a productive spermstud. What would you like to see first?"

"I don't know. What do you recommend?"

"Do you like to swim?" he asked.

"Yes, I do. I learned to swim when I was a boy, on Earth."

"Well, I had to learn in an artificial pool, because I grew up on the Moon, where water was very expensive. But here there's a swimming pool on each floor. Let's go."

We walked out into the corridor. The 0800 shift was being called on the speakers. "0800 extractor shift...0800 extractor shift..." Men in black tunics were hurrying back and forth. Bron and I reached a set of double doors marked POOL. The doors slid open to reveal a huge pool filled with blue-green water and surrounded by generous walkways covered with soft black plastoid.

"No formalities here," Bron said, throwing his tunic onto one of the benches that lined the walls and slipping off his boots. I did the same. He dived into the limpid green water, and I followed him. The water was as warm as mother's milk. Through the ripples caused by our movements, I could see his big mule dick bobbing between his legs.

"This is wonderful, isn't it?" he said.

"I never expected to find a swimming pool in the asteroid belt," I replied, laughing.

We swam for a long time in silence, then clambered out of the pool to lay on the soft black plastoid. Solar lamps overhead warmed our naked bodies. Bron reclined on his back, his enormous donkey meat stretched out at a crazy angle across his muscular thigh. His legs were spread slightly apart, and his mammoth testicles hung down to rest on the plastoid floor like two pears in a sack. I couldn't keep my eyes off his sexual equipment. I had never seen anything so impressive. His physique was stunning too. I couldn't help propping myself up on one elbow and staring up and down the length of his body, the pale white Lunarian skin gleaming with droplets of water, the silvery hairs sparkling in the light of the solar lamps.

He sensed what I was thinking. "Pretty amazing, isn't it?" he said. "It's the hormones that do it. Wait a few weeks, and you'll begin to look this way too. And after a while the effect becomes permanent. There's no going back, whether you like it or not."

"Oh, I like it," I said. "I like it."

I lay back and put my head on my hands and stared up at the ceiling, daydreaming about having a huge dick hanging between my legs and a pair of nuts the size of navel oranges dangling halfway to my knees.

After lunch in the restaurant, Bron said, "Let's go to the holodisc library and get something to watch."

We took the pneumolift to the first level. The library was a large room packed with shelves holding thousands of discs. Bron reached up to an upper shelf and pulled one down.

"This is one of my favorites," he said. "Let's go to my cube, and I'll play it for you."

As soon as we entered his room and the door slid shut, Bron threw off his tunic. I followed suit. He motioned for me to sit in one of the two pneumochairs, then slid the disc into the player, pressed the start button, and sat down in the other chair. We both stared as the wall seemed to disappear and there formed an Earth scene of a waterfall on a tropical island. In the water were frolicking three young native women. They splashed water at each other and playfully shoved and pushed while occasionally fondling each other's nipples and lightly kissing each other on the lips or on the ears or on the back of the neck.

"This really turns me on," said Bron.

I supposed it was because opposites attract. He was so large, so tall, his skin so pale, and these little creatures of the holodisc were small and dark-haired, their skin deep and tawny.

For the first time, I saw Bron's mule dick begin to grow, and, I must say, I was quite stunned. It slowly began to swell as he watched the frolicking girls. Soon he began to stroke it without shame. It rose to its full, massive proportions, with a rosy head the size of a large plum and a rigid, veined pink shaft that reached almost up to the nipples on his chest. His hands were big, but when he closed his fist around his cock, he could not make his fingers meet. There was plenty of room on the shaft for both his hands, and he used them both, stroking up and down, sometimes in the same direction, sometimes in opposite directions.

My own dick began to grow hard despite the fact that it had been so thoroughly drained the day before. I guessed that it must be the hormones promoting this relentless sex drive.

The Guardian Angel in the center of the room began to whir and buzz. Suddenly a metallic voice burst out from the mouth-piece of the robot: "No unauthorized orgasms! No unauthorized orgasms!"

The Angel floated down toward Bron's stroking hands and grabbed his wrists, pulling them apart.

"No unauthorized orgasms!" it repeated.

"That's the way it is," Bron said, shaking his head and sighing. "I've heard of some studs who've figured out a way to bypass the Angels, but I have yet to learn how it's done. I'll have to see if I can find out, because I sure would like to jerk off right now."

I looked down at my own dick. It was hard and throbbing but less than half the size of Bron's. "So would I," I lamented.

"Well, we can just sit and watch," he said. So we sat and watched the entire holodisc, which lasted almost an hour, our pricks all the while throbbing with hormone-stimulated lust. The Guardian Angel floated in the center of the room, whirring and buzzing, ever vigilant against unauthorized sperm release.

DAY TWELVE

It was the day after my fourth stint on the extractor. I had had the experience of lying in a room with twenty other spermstuds, each of us a passive subject on this semen production line. But in the insular world of the neorotransmitter helmets, we each experienced our own private universe of orgasmic brinkmanship. Everyone else seemed to take the procedures for granted, and the strangeness was wearing off for me as well. I looked forward to my next session on the machines and to the experience of heightened, prolonged sexual ecstasy.

I awoke early, at 0700 hours. I felt wide awake and alert but as if I were lacking something. I put on my tunic and went to the shower stalls. As I looked at myself in the mirrored walls of the shower room, I could notice a remarkable effect. The hormones had caused my muscles to begin to fill out. I had never been thin, but now muscles were beginning to stand out in high relief, as if the hormones were somehow pumping them up.

Next I looked at my penis hanging between my legs and at my balls dangling behind it. I hadn't taken any measurements, but I could tell just by looking that my cock was definitely longer and thicker and my balls had certainly increased in size. I stepped into the shower, and immediately hot water began to tingle all over my body. I felt very alert, almost on edge. I felt I needed something, but I didn't know what exactly. I felt hungry in a way that I couldn't describe.

After my shower I stepped into the air dryer, where tiny jets of warm air evaporated the droplets of water off my body. Then I put on my tunic and walked over to the restaurant. I was hungry—very, very hungry. Much hungrier than usual.

I looked around. Bron was at our regular table. He gave me a big smile as I sat down.

"I'm so hungry, I could eat an alien," I said.

He looked at me inquisitively. He was drinking coffee and eating one of the hormone-laced omelettes. I waved an Angel over to the table. I had learned the ropes. "Coffee; two eggs, scrambled; bacon; and biscuits with honey." I was famished. The Angel waiter hurried away.

"You're still liking getting juiced?" Bron asked. "Yesterday was your fourth stint, wasn't it?"

"Sure do," I answered. "And yesterday was the best ever. I'm actually looking forward to it now."

"You'd better watch yourself," Bron said, "or you'll find yourself signing up for another three-month contract."

"Yeah, I'm beginning to have some thoughts about that."

The Angel placed my breakfast before me, and I devoured it greedily. A few minutes later my plate was empty.

But oddly enough I still felt hungry. I looked around the room as if seeking an answer to this peculiar empty feeling.

"I think I'm still hungry," I said, turning to Bron.

He looked at me quizzically. His expression seemed worried. "Hungry in what way?" he inquired.

"I don't know," I replied. "I've had a lot of food. I just feel like I'm hungry for something, but I don't know what it is."

Bron stared into my eyes for a long time before he finally spoke. "What would you say if I said that you wanted sperm?" There was a very long silence while we both stared at each other.

Finally I said, "Sperm?"

"Yes," Bron answered, still looking into my eyes. "Sperm. Is that what you want?"

At first I couldn't believe my ears. Then it gradually sunk in. I thought about the vial of my own sperm that Zschado had held in his hands the day I arrived on Xenobia. I thought about putting it to my lips and drinking it. But that wasn't exactly right. No, not my own sperm. I wanted the sperm of another man. I wanted fresh hot sperm directly from another man's cock!

I couldn't believe what I was thinking! I put my head in my hands and massaged my temples. I stared down at the remains of my breakfast.

"It's true then," said Bron. "That is what you want, isn't it?"

"I...I don't know," I replied. I lifted my head and looked at him again.

"I'm afraid," he began, "that I have bad news for you, Antony, my friend. I think you've come down with sperm hunger."

"What's that?" I gasped. "What's sperm hunger?"

Bron looked at me sorrowfully. "It's a peculiar effect of the extraction process. I've heard about it, but I've never seen anyone get it. I hear it's an insatiable hunger for fresh sperm from another man's dick, and nothing else will satisfy it. I've heard that it happens to about one spermstud in a hundred. People don't talk much about it because everyone's afraid of it. I've also heard that sometimes it lasts for a few days and sometimes for weeks and weeks, until your body adjusts to the hormones and to the extraction process."

"Damn it!" I said, putting my face into my hands again and gritting my teeth. "What the hell am I going to do?"

He sounded sympathetic. "I don't think there's much you can do, Antony, except grin and bear it. I hate to say that, but I know there's no cure."

Without another word, I rose from the table and stormed through the doors and into the corridor.

The last extractor shift of the day was just ending, and studs of all descriptions were moving through the hall, many of them with large postextraction hard-ons showing beneath their tunics. I couldn't help staring at their erect sex tools—I realized now that this was what I needed to have. I needed to get some fresh sperm to satisfy this gnawing hunger.

My stomach was contracting. My throat felt dry and parched. I licked my lips involuntarily, staring at this parade of hot male meat. I walked in a daze around the full circumference of Xenobia several times, and finally I pushed open the rest-room doors and went into the urinal.

A tall dark-haired stud was standing beside the large funnel. His beautiful dick trembled as he shook the last drops of urine from the glistening tip. I stood next to him. I couldn't help staring down at his cock, and finally I reached out my hand and began to stroke his big, meaty man tool.

He smiled faintly and looked into my eyes sympathetically. "What's up, friend?" he asked.

"Excuse me, sir, but could I suck your dick, please?"

He frowned a bit, then began to fasten his tunic. "Sorry, buster, I just got off the extractor about an hour ago. Maybe some other time." He turned on his heel and walked out into the corridor.

I felt my cheeks go red with shame as I replayed in my mind what I had just done. I had actually asked another man if I could suck his penis! Part of me was outraged at this strange behavior, and yet another part of me—the part that was experiencing the sperm hunger—was deeply moved, eager for another encounter with a throbbing cock.

As I stood there, my mind going numb with confusion, the door to the corridor opened, and another spermstud entered the urinal room. He walked to the railing a few paces away and began to unfasten his tunic, taking out a massive dick and beginning to piss. I gazed hungrily at his huge man meat as his golden stream cascaded down the funnel. When he was finished he stood there for a few moments.

I couldn't help myself. I walked over and looked greedily at his gorgeous cock. I licked my lips. I looked into his eyes.

"Please, sir," I pleaded, "may I suck your dick? Please?"

He raised an eyebrow scornfully. "Too bad, mate," he said. "That's not my thing. But keep trying. Maybe you'll have better luck next time." He shook his huge dick several times as if to cruelly tempt me with the unattainable. Then he fastened his tunic and left the room.

My cheeks were red again. I was so ashamed. I rushed out into the corridor. I had to find someone...someone who could help me satisfy this terrible, obscene craving. I wandered the corridors of Xenobia for several hours, my stomach in knots and my mouth and throat dry and parched. My eyes almost bulged out of my head every time I passed a stud with a hard-on.

Finally I ended up in front of my own cubicle. I lay down on the bed and stared at the ceiling. What could I do? I couldn't go into anyone's room or ask anyone to my room; the Guardian Angels would prevent any unauthorized sperm release! The only place seemed to be the urinals, and I had no luck there. Where could I go? Whom could I turn to?

Dr. Sax! He could help me! I sprang off the bunk and rushed out into the corridor. I ran to room 606. The sign on the door read DR. AUGUSTUS SAX. I knocked gingerly. Dr. Sax's voice said, "Come in," as the door slid open.

He was seated behind his desk. He looked up and smiled as I entered. The door shut behind me.

"Dr. Sax," I said, "I need your help. Please."

He looked at me with deep concern. "What's wrong, my boy?"

"Dr. Sax, I have the sperm hunger."

His eyes widened. "Oh, my dear, I'm so sorry! Tell me, how did it happen? When did it happen?"

"I woke up this morning feeling odd. Then, after breakfast, I was still hungry. My friend Bron—I mean, Spermstud 660—figured out what was wrong with me. He explained to me what he had learned through hearsay about it after I told him how peculiar I was feeling. And then I couldn't help myself. I approached several men and asked them if I could...could...if I could suck their dicks," I finally managed to say. "I really need sperm badly, Dr. Sax. I need it so badly that I can't tell you how badly I need it. I need it so bad."

Dr. Sax came around the desk and patted me on the shoulder. "My boy, you have no idea how sorry I am to hear that you have come down with this strange ailment."

I looked down to see that his cock was erect beneath his white smock. I couldn't help myself. I reached down and began to massage his dick through the smock.

"Dr. Sax, please—may I suck your dick?"

In answer, he undid his smock and pulled it back. Then he unfastened his loose-fitting trousers to reveal a very large, erect, and throbbing penis.

I fell to my knees, trembling, and placed the swollen red tip of his cock between my lips. There was no Guardian Angel in the room to prevent me from having my way with this man's beautiful dick. I began to lick and suck on the head of it. The sperm hunger drove me further and further so that I wanted to plunge the entire length of it down my throat. But this was impossible because it was much too large. So I grasped the base with both hands instead, massaging the swollen shaft with short up-and-down motions.

Dr. Sax's penis was of such impressive size that I figured he had once been a spermstud himself. His dick responded to my sucking and massaging by becoming even harder and more distended. The veins stood out on the shaft, and the head grew smooth and shiny. I slurped and sucked on it, moving my right hand up and down the shaft while my left hand massaged his massive testicles, which soon began to tighten as if to release their load of hot sperm.

"Go ahead, my boy, enjoy yourself!" gasped Dr. Sax. "You are one of my favorite spermstuds, and it is a pleasure to be able to relieve your hunger as best I can." His breath was ragged. "Since we have not been able to isolate the factors that cause sperm hunger or discover a remedy, this donation of my own seed is the least I can do for you!"

He grasped the back of my head and pulled me farther down on his stiff come rod. Soon he was fucking my face without mercy, groaning and heaving in preorgasmic tension. His pelvis thrust forward as he pushed my head down until I was about to vomit. But suddenly, mercifully, a hot stream of come poured down my parched throat. Spurt after spurt of salty sperm followed the first as I sucked and slurped even more vigorously, swallowing greedily until I had drained Dr. Sax's cock of every last drop of delicious, creamy man seed that he had to offer. His dick began to soften a bit in my mouth, and finally he withdrew.

I sat back on my haunches and looked up at him to see a satisfied smile on his face. He patted my cheek with one beefy hand. "I hope this makes you feel better, my boy."

"Yes, Dr. Sax," I replied. "Yes, it does. I feel much, much better." I rose to my feet, somewhat in a daze, and said, "Thank you, Dr. Sax. Thank you so much." Then I turned and left his office.

It was late. I had wandered around all day. I had had my first taste of another man's sperm. I felt lethargic, exhausted. I returned to my cube, collapsed on the bunk, and fell into a deep, dreamless sleep.

DAY THIRTEEN

I woke up feeling invigorated yet afraid—afraid of the sperm hunger, afraid of what it would do to me. I felt myself changing into something unfamiliar, unknown, dangerous. I felt hungry again. I felt the same way I had the day before.

I hurried to the restaurant and ordered a huge breakfast, which I devoured frantically. But it didn't satisfy the hunger. I knew it wouldn't. It was going to be the same as yesterday.

Shit! I thought. *It's happening again. I need...I need a dick! I need a big, fat, juicy dick! And I need it bad!*

I hastened over to Dr. Sax's office, visualizing his massive sex meat. As I approached, however, I saw a small sign posted on the door. It read DR. SAX WILL BE ON VACATION UNTIL FURTHER NOTICE. I stared in amazed disappointment. Now what would I do? Whom could I turn to?

Out of desperation I decided to go see Zschado. As much as I was afraid of him, perhaps he could give me information, advice, help—anything. At this point I was grasping at straws.

The door marked z slid open. Zschado sat at his desk, making calculations on a keypad. He looked up as I entered. "Well, well, Spermstud 677, what can I do for you?"

I crossed over to the desk and looked him straight in the eyes. "Zschado," I said, "I have the sperm hunger."

In spite of his cool demeanor, his eyes widened visibly. He did not smile his customary sardonic smile. "Well," he said thoughtfully. "Hmm..."

"You've got to help me, Zschado," I pleaded. "This is something you didn't tell me about. It's not part of the contract."

Now he smiled. "I never said there wouldn't be some risk," he pointed out. "But this is very unusual! It seldom happens."

"Seldom or not, I need help!" I yelled. "I'm going crazy, Zschado!"

"Well, there's no cure—you know that, Spermstud 677. I'm afraid the only thing I can do is to help you get some sperm."

"Would you?" I asked. I felt an immense sense of relief.

"Well, yes, I could. And it would be hot and fresh." He looked directly at me, his eyes boring into mine. "Hot and fresh!" he repeated.

I felt myself blushing again, but I couldn't help repeating his words. "Yes, yes!" I said excitedly. "Hot and fresh! Please!"

"Very well, then," he said. He pushed a button on his desk console and spoke into an intercom. "MacGogg, come to me." After a few moments the back door behind Zschado's desk opened. I surmised that it must be the entryway to the secret precincts of Xenobia. From this doorway emerged a giant blond mutant.

MacGogg was a head taller than Zschado and covered all over with soft, curly golden hair. His pale blue eyes stared blankly into the distance. He towered two heads above me.

"Remove tunic, MacGogg," Zschado instructed. MacGogg slipped his tunic from his shoulders, and it fell to the floor at his feet, revealing an astonishing piece of sexual equipment between his legs—a pole of enormous proportions.

"Now," Zschado said, turning to me, "tell MacGogg what you need, and he will give it to you. The only thing is, he doesn't particularly like to be touched. So you must convince him to give you what you need by having him manipulate himself, without your actual physical assistance. You see, MacGogg is my personal spermstud."

I looked up into MacGogg's blank face. His soft blue eyes stared without blinking. "MacGogg," I began tentatively, "give me your sperm." The giant stood there and did nothing. I looked at Zschado, who smiled and shook his head.

"Come now, Spermstud 677, you must be more persuasive with MacGogg. He's not very bright. Tell him what you need and why you need it. Tell him how magnificent he is. Maybe that would work." A cruel smile played on Zschado's full red lips. "You might even try getting down on your knees. But not too close, you understand."

I sank to my knees. I was staring directly at MacGogg's huge, fleshy come cannon. It swung heavily from his groin only a meter away from my parched lips, tantalizing me with its promise of hot, fresh sperm.

I began to plead. "O great MacGogg, your humble servant begs you for fresh, hot sperm." My cheeks were reddening with the shame of what I was doing. Tears came to my eyes at the thought of how much come that magnificent organ would be able to produce to sate my hunger.

I continued my prayers to MacGogg. "O magnificent MacGogg, owner of the greatest organ on Xenobia, your servant begs you for hot, fresh sperm. Your servant has the sperm hunger, which only you can satisfy..." My supplications seemed to be working. The mutant's giant tool began to stir. "O magnificent MacGogg," I continued, "whose organ is the greatest in the universe, your servant begs you for hot, fresh sperm to soothe his parched, sperm-hungry throat. O great MacGogg, stroke your mighty organ and release the seed of life for your hungry servant!"

MacGogg's blank blue eyes still stared into the distance, but his organ was growing noticeably more erect. His right arm moved upward and began to stroke the mighty shaft while his left hand began to knead the huge apple-red glans. Soon his massive member stood at full height, towering above my head, a singing skyscraper of sexual energy.

MacGogg's huge hands began to pound his massive meat as my supplications continued. "O mighty MacGogg, all powerful master of Phallos, shower your servant with your blessings—fill his hungry throat with your plentiful seed. Stroke your gigantic sex pole until the entire universe is covered with your male milk. Hear my prayer, mighty MacGogg!"

The giant mutant's hands moved rhythmically over his huge cock. I gazed hungrily up at the tip, waiting for the sperm to begin pouring out.

MacGogg began to pound his meat even more furiously. "Great MacGogg," I intoned, "shower me with your gifts...send your hot, fresh sperm to your servant!" I was almost shouting.

Immediately gobs of sperm began to erupt from the tip of his engorged man meat. "Spread out your hands!" ordered Zschado. "Catch the sperm as it comes for you."

I cupped my hands below MacGogg's massive member and watched as fresh, steaming sperm fell into my palms. I began to eat it hungrily, trying not to waste a moment as each new eruption poured forth from MacGogg's incredible phallus. Blast after blast of hot sperm shot into my outstretched palms, and I licked them greedily as more and more poured out—an amazing amount of sperm. I gobbled down a full meal, and still more came. It dropped on the floor and ran down my arms. I bent over and licked it off the floor while it was still warm. I licked it off my arms. Gobs splashed on top of my head. How I longed to fasten my mouth directly on the source of this bounty, but I was afraid to disobey Zschado's warning.

All too soon the feast was over, and I sat back, sated. MacGogg's hands dropped away from his spent penis, his blue eyes still staring blankly into the distance.

"Thank MacGogg for his gifts," Zschado said.

I licked my sticky lips. "O great MacGogg, thank you for your bountiful seed. Thank you!"

"MacGogg may leave," Zschado said, handing the mutant his tunic. MacGogg slipped the tunic over his massive frame, then turned and exited through the interior door and into the secret precincts of Xenobia, where Zschado hid, I felt sure, many more strange and wondrous things.

I leaned over and licked up the last remaining puddles of sperm from the floor. I could not resist.

"Very good," said Zschado. "I hope I have been of some assistance. I am always glad to do a spermstud a favor. You understand that MacGogg's sperm is of no use to the aliens because he is a mutant. You could tell, I am sure, from his size and coloring that he is not an ordinary human being. His ancestors were among those exposed to gamma radiation back in year 73—that unfortunate accident on Mars colony. Perhaps you remember hearing of that affair—of the implosion of the fusion reactor.

Because of that, his DNA structure is abnormal. At any rate, even though the aliens are not interested in his sperm, some humans still find it, shall we say, enjoyable." He smiled sarcastically as he stroked the bulge in his armored trousers.

"You may go now," he said.

DAY FIFTEEN

The morning after my fifth session on the extractor found me ravenous once again with the sperm hunger. I felt physically energized, alert, and exceedingly horny—the effects of the megahormones, no doubt. But at the same time, a sense of despair overwhelmed my mind. I needed hot, fresh sperm again. Where could I find what I needed above all else?

I couldn't face the humiliation of worshiping before the cock of MacGogg again. I lay on my bunk in a fury of frustration, my mind racing. Then the solution came to me. It was in the next cubicle! Room 678! The spermstud who had grabbed my arm in the restaurant and invited me to his room.

I slipped on my tunic, stepped into the corridor, and knocked. The door slid open.

"Well, cutie," Spermstud 678 said, "what brings you to my door?" He was lying on his bed reading a book, his hard-on clearly visible beneath his tunic. He propped himself up on one elbow to look at me.

I was somewhat at a loss for words. "I...I'm Antony," I stuttered, "Spermstud 677. I—"

"I'm Menelik," he interrupted, beckoning me inside. "Come in, damn it! Don't stand in the corridor!"

The door slid shut behind me, and I was alone with Menelik. I decided to be direct. "I have the sperm hunger, Menelik. I need...I need..."

"So that's your story, huh? Well, cutie, let me wise you up. I've been in space a long time. I could tell you things about men and sperm that would make your hair curl. Do you know who gets the sperm hunger?"

I shook my head. "No," I admitted. I was almost afraid to ask.

He looked me up and down cynically. "I'll tell you. I can spot a fag a light-year away. It's guys like you who won't admit that they want sex with other men who get the sperm hunger. All those hormones along with the suspended orgasms on the extractor stir up the unresolved shit in your psyche. All the repressed urges come to the surface, demanding to be satisfied."

He paused and looked at me meaningfully. I looked down at the floor and let Menelik's message sink in. Could he be right? Had I really wanted men all these years? I looked up to see him smiling.

"Let's get down to the point," he said. "I've known a few spermstuds who have come down with the sperm hunger, and there's one sure cure. It's not eating sperm. That just satisfies the craving temporarily. To get cured permanently, you have to get a good load of hot, fresh come delivered directly into your back door, deep into your guts. That's the cure."

I could see a growing bulge beneath his tunic. His coppery skin glowed with sex energy.

"I figure you know what you really want," he continued, "and what you really want is for me to shove my big hard dick up your ass. That's what you want, isn't it?"

"I...I..." I stammered.

"Cut the crap! Come on, get your ass over the back of the pneumochair."

"But..." I protested, "what about...?" With a tilt of my head, I indicated the Guardian Angel floating near the ceiling.

Menelik laughed. "No problem," he said, slipping off his tunic. With an expert flip of his arm, he tossed the garment over the floating robot. "There," he said. "Nighty-night. They're quite stupid—they can do only what they're programmed to do. It thinks I've turned out the lights." He chuckled mischievously.

The robot floated quietly near the ceiling on its antigravs, the black tunic covering its body. It looked like an ebony ghost.

I examined Menelik's naked body. His stocky frame bulged with heavy, knotted muscles rippling beneath his hairless, copper-colored skin. His formidable battering ram stood out from his loins as big as my forearm, the huge purple head as hard as a man's fist.

He pulled off my tunic and looked at my naked body. "I like new studs like you with little dicks." He grabbed my shoulders and pushed me toward the pneumochair. He bent me over the back of the chair with my ass sticking up. The chair adjusted to my weight, and I was balanced there, my virgin rectum pointing directly at Menelik's rigid man tool. It stood away from his body and glowed like a red-hot poker. His heavy gonads swung like lead weights.

"Like I said, I've been in space a long time," he told me. "I like my sex raw, not dressed up with lace panties and vanilla eau de cologne." He spit on one hand and rubbed the saliva into my anus. He positioned his massive cock head against my helpless bung hole.

A shock ran through my entire frame as Menelik, without further ado, shoved his rigid ramrod halfway into my unsuspecting virgin anus. A scream issued from my throat.

"Good thing the Guardian Angels don't mind people screaming," he remarked under his breath as he shoved his prong deeper into my tortured guts. In another moment I felt his hips grinding against my butt cheeks, and I knew that he now had the full length of his cock in my unprepared ass channel. Screams of agony continued to erupt from my throat.

"Good thing these cubicles are soundproofed," he muttered as he pulled out halfway and then shoved his blaster in again to the hilt. More screams and moans ripped from my throat.

"Maybe I'll have to gag you," he said, chuckling.

Menelik ground his penetrator deep into my intestines. Gradually the agony subsided and became simply a brilliant flame that darted from my anus to somewhere deep within my body. Menelik thrust in and out, his strong, stocky body driving his massive truncheon deeper and deeper into my ass. I held on to the pneumochair for dear life as he ruthlessly fucked my butt like a veteran rider breaking in an inexperienced colt.

All too soon Menelik heaved a great gasp, and I felt a torrid spurt of sticky sperm coating my entrails, deep inside my torso. Immediately, with an agile backward movement, he withdrew his steely pole completely from my hole and then, in an instant, shoved it back in again. Another geyser of hot lava erupted into my intestines.

He pulled out again. I waited breathlessly for the ultimate assault. Then it came.

He viciously plunged his warhead for the third time deeper than he had penetrated before, delivering a final payload of thick, hot man sap deep into the most profound recesses of my battered guts.

Then, with deft up-and-down movements, he gradually wiggled his long come cannon around until the massive head was poised against my prostate. He flexed his knees and pressed hard, and my own rigid dick erupted in torrents of jism, coating the pneumochair.

"Don't tell me I don't know how to fuck!" he chortled. "I've learned a lot of things in space, and that's one of them."

He withdrew his prick and wiped it on a towel. He gave a perfunctory wipe on my throbbing asshole, then threw the towel into the disposal chute. He grabbed my shoulders and pulled me up from the chair.

"Here's your tunic," he said, helping me slip it on. "Look, I like you. I think you're a real cutie. So if you need some more help, just knock on my door."

He pushed me out into the corridor. "See ya real soon." He waved his hand. The door slid shut.

I stood there—my knees trembling and my slimy, sperm-coated intestines throbbing and burning—staring at the door marked 678. I realized that I had much to learn from Menelik. It would take a while to absorb this new self-awareness. I turned and walked toward the shower stalls to wash my sticky skin. In spite of my bodily discomfort, my mind was clear. I was extremely happy.

The sperm hunger was gone.

DAY SIXTEEN

I spent the morning practicing flipping my tunic over the Guardian Angel in my cube. After an hour or so, I was as expert as Menelik. With an easy upward movement of my arm, I could invariably cover the robot without a second try. This little trick would, I was sure, come in handy.

The sperm hunger was definitely gone. It had been replaced by a new awareness of myself and of my sexuality. I decided to act on this new knowledge by visiting Bron. I had not seen him since that day in the restaurant when he had diagnosed my sperm hunger. He was my only true friend on Xenobia. He had been kind to me from the first moment I met him.

I knocked on door 660, Bron's cube. As the door slid open, I saw Bron sitting dejectedly on his bunk, staring at the floor. He raised his head. His eyes were red and wet from weeping.

I sat beside him on the bunk and put my arm around his massive shoulders. "Bron, what's the matter?"

He handed me a thin blue tissue, which I realized was an ethernote. "Read this," he said, sniffling. "It's from Moira, my woman on Lunacolony. She's leaving me for someone else."

I read the ethernote hastily:

> *Dear Bron,*
> *There is no reason to pretend that our relationship can continue. You should not have mailed me that picture of your organs, showing the enlargement that has occurred. They are unnatural and grotesque. No woman in her right mind would want a man who is as deformed as you are now. I am taking the children and moving to Earth. I have met a nice older man who has a farm in Iowa.*
>
> *Regretfully, Moira*

"Oh, Bron, I'm so sorry," I said, squeezing his shoulders with my arm.

He sniffed and rubbed his eyes. "I told you that once the enlargement process starts, there's no going back. Now Moira thinks I'm a freak. I thought she'd be pleased, but she thinks I'm grotesque and deformed. I hate my big donkey dick. I hate my huge testicles. I hate Xenobia. I hate hormones. I hate myself for getting into this in the first place." He put his face in his hands.

"Bron," I murmured, "I like you the way you are." I massaged his shoulder with my left hand, and with my right hand I began to rub his thigh tenderly. "I love your tall, muscled, beautiful white body. I love your immense white mule dick. I love your big, heavy balls. I love everything about you, Bron."

The fabric of his tunic began to lift as his big cock began to stir. I pulled back the fabric and watched in awe as this huge meat column slowly swelled and stood at attention. I stroked it gently for a few minutes, listening to Bron's breathing deepen and quicken as a sexual energy took hold of his body. I slid my tunic from my body and expertly flipped it over the Guardian Angel floating above. Bron smiled in spite of his grief. "So that's how it's done—so simple."

I gently pushed his big torso back so that he was reclining against the pillow. I went down on my knees between his powerful thighs. "Let me make you feel good, Bron," I whispered. He closed his eyes, as if in agreement, and relaxed with a sigh.

He moaned as I began to flick my hot tongue over the deep pink head of his cock. The urethral slot was so large that I could fit the tip of my tongue inside, giving it a passionate French kiss. I closed my lips over the entire head, large as a crab apple, my tongue sliding in and out of the big come hole. The rhythm of his breathing increased, and he spread his muscular thighs and thrust his pelvis upward. Perhaps he was thinking of Moira's hot, wet pussy as I attempted to slide his fuck tool farther and farther down my eager throat.

His engorged shaft, resembling a sturdy white marble column laced with pink veins, glowed in the soft light of the cubicle. My loneliness and isolation of the past few weeks dissolved as I made love to this beautiful Lunarian being, savoring his deep moans and sighs.

There was no way to take it all. His tool was much thicker and longer than even Menelik's. I grasped the heavy shaft with both hands. My fingers could not meet around the massive girth of it. I squeezed and massaged the base while I tried my best to swallow as much of its length as I was able.

I realized that I was deeply in love with Bron. All my life seemed to be a preparation for this act of giving pleasure. I raised my eyes to drink in the glory of his massively muscled, alabasterlike body: the soft, silvery hair; his head thrown back on the pillow; the parted lips from which issued deep, ecstatic breathing. My newfound sexuality blossomed in waves of sympathetic pleasure that rushed through my body in burning surges. Why had I denied my attraction to men all these years? The tears streaming from my eyes were only partially caused by the effort to force his rigid pole down my throat.

I wanted to impale myself on this magnificent come machine. I tried to gag myself by forcing it down my throat and into my esophagus. I pulled Bron's bull meat down at a different angle so that I could get more of its impossible length into my pussy mouth. My feelings of animal lust for this gorgeous man drove me into a sucking frenzy!

Somehow I managed to press my head down past the gag point, and I felt the indescribable sensation of his engorged cock head entering my esophagus. I rose up off my knees to a better angle of entry.

I abandoned all caution. Holding tight with both hands to the shaft of this towering pile driver, I took one last deep breath and plunged my face down like a diver into a pool of water. His big dick head slid down my esophagus like an oiled piston. My head reeled with the lust of this penetration into previously virgin tissue, and soon I felt the reward of blasts of white-hot sperm against the walls of my esophagus. Gasping with orgasmic delight, Bron inadvertently thrust his pelvis upward at the first spurts of come. This deeper penetration was too much for my inexperienced throat, and I began to gag. I pulled my head back to watch the spectacle of Bron's continuing sperm shoot. I still held the turgid shaft with both hands. I sank back to my knees, his spurting cock inches from my face. His huge white dick throbbed like some mighty machine as it spewed forth gobs of cream, twitching and pulsating in my fists. Great moans heaved from his lips. After many spumes of jism landed on his stomach and thighs, my massaging hands brought forth the final low-energy pulses of flowing come, which ran down the shaft, then over my hands and forearms. His huge, tightened testicles slowly began to relax.

I watched his jizz flow down the tree-trunk shaft, and I began to lick it off delicately, as if it were a sweet and tasty sap—nature's own nectar. I cleaned the shaft completely with my tongue, then licked clean my fingers and wrists. Finally I sucked up the fallen gobs of delicious cream from his belly and thighs.

Bron's heavy breaths gradually subsided. His eyes opened.

"That was wonderful, Bron, just wonderful," I sighed.

He stared at me for a moment. "That was my first time," he said. "That was the first time I have had sexual intimacy with another man." His face seemed blank, betraying neither censure nor delight.

"Please go now," he said. "I want to think about Moira. I want to think about what to do next."

I stood and looked lovingly at Bron's magnificent body, at his softening penis lying across his thigh like a fallen tree, at his handsome face with its enigmatic expression. I reached up and slipped my tunic from the floating Guardian Angel. There seemed to be nothing to say. I went out the door into the corridor without looking back.

I needed time to think too.

DAY EIGHTEEN

My sixth session on the extractor had been both excruciating and ecstatic. Afterward I had taken a light dinner and had fallen into my bed for a deep, heavy sleep. Now, in the soft light of my cubicle, on my eighteenth "morning" by Xenobia's artificial clocks, I examined my body again in the retractable mirror. My musculature, now hard and sinewy, had the appearance of someone who had spent years training with pneumoweights. My penis and testicles were definitely larger, thicker, and heavier. The megahormones had permeated every cell and molecule of my body. My testicles, in particular, hung well below my groin. Heavy with sperm, they seemed almost like the udders of a milk-laden cow. (*Does a cow being milked feel the intense pleasure that I feel on the extractor?* I smiled at the thought.) And though I had just been on the extractor machine the day before, I saw that my balls were already swollen with the fresh sperm my hormone-laden body had manufactured during the night.

I was also incredibly horny. The damned hormones worked on the mind as well as the body. I thought of Bron and his sorrowful mood. Was it too soon to attempt to see him again? It had been two days, and I yearned to be close to his magnificent body, but I was afraid of his possible rejection. My daydream of Bron was interrupted by a message on the speaker in my cubicle. "Spermstud 677! Spermstud 677! You are wanted in Dr. Sax's office immediately!"

What now? I thought as I pulled on my tunic and boots. A few minutes later I stood in front of a smiling Dr. Sax. He motioned for me to have a seat.

"This is a unique occasion, 677," he began. "I must first tell you that your sperm-production levels are the highest in the twelve-year history of Xenobia." He glanced approvingly at my crotch. My balls twitched at the thought—I was spermstud numero uno!

"You are going to meet an alien, Mr. Stout," Dr. Sax continued. My mouth fell open, and my eyes bulged.

"I feel that I must use your actual name," he added, "contrary to the protocol of Xenobia, for this is such a unique occasion that it warrants special behavior. Let me explain." He settled back in his pneumochair and placed his beefy fingers together.

"Your sperm production has been so extraordinary that the aliens—the Vronks—have expressed a desire to meet you face-to-face. In fact, they are so eager to make contact with you that they have authorized us to double your contract salary. So if you agree, your payment will be 700 million universal credits at the end of your stint on Xenobia. Of course, you may sign up again for another three months if you desire."

My brain was spinning with this new information. *When? Why? Where?* I closed my eyes for a few moments to compose my thoughts. "OK, I agree," I said finally. "When will the meeting take place?"

Dr. Sax smiled in satisfaction. "A very wise decision, Mr. Stout. You will profit greatly from this meeting." He took a cyberpad from his desktop and studied it for a few moments. "We will arrange a meeting with the Vronk for the day after tomorrow. This appointment will take the place of your usual shift on the extractor. You will arrive at Zschado's office at 0800 hours. The meeting will be held there. You will spend approximately four hours with the Vronk.

"You have been greatly honored, Mr. Stout," he continued. "Only a very few human beings have met the aliens face-to-face. I myself have seen them on only six occasions, for our business dealings. All other times they communicate by ethernote in mathematical code."

He looked at me sternly. "And I must warn you not to reveal this meeting to anyone else on Xenobia," he said. "It must be absolutely secret! Do you understand?"

"Yes, I understand, Dr. Sax."

"Very well, then. But before you go, I should like to examine you. Come here and remove your tunic."

I stood before Dr. Sax and let my tunic fall to the floor. He reached out and took my cock in his big strong hands. He kneaded it with his fingers. "Your genital enlargement is proceeding unusually fast," he said. My pole began to stiffen under the good doctor's expert stimulation. He looked at me with a twinkle in his eye. "How is the sperm hunger? Still bothering you?"

Did he expect another suck job? "The sperm hunger is gone, Dr. Sax." I thought of Menelik's pounding my virgin bung hole to provide the cure. My rigid cock twitched at the memory.

"Have you been having any unauthorized sperm emissions?" he queried.

"No, Dr. Sax," I lied. "Never."

He hefted my swollen testicles, one in each hand. "Ah! Your sperm recovery rate is exceptional. If you don't mind, I'd like to give you some direct megahormone injections."

I nodded agreement. What would have happened had I said no?

He took up a syringe filled with pale green liquid. It was my first look at the synthetic hormones in their pure state, unmixed with food or drink. My horny man pole was now standing at full attention, pointing upward and throbbing. Dr. Sax placed the tip of the syringe firmly at the base of my erection and pushed the pressure button. The hormone solution blasted its way through the epidermis directly into the muscular tissue beneath. A tingling, burning sensation suffused my engorged penis. He lifted my left testicle. A second syringe full of megahormones blasted through the sac directly into my already swollen gonad. A third injection to the right gonad completed the treatment. I groaned in agony.

My balls burned like fire, and as they fell from Dr. Sax's hands, they felt like lead weights, pulling down from my groin. My dick throbbed and ached. He looked at his handiwork with satisfaction. "Good," he muttered. "Good."

He handed me a small plastoid parcel containing a pinch of pink powder. "You may expect this erection to last for a few hours. You will sleep better if you take this medication before you retire tonight. Call me in the morning if you have any problems." He smiled winningly. "I'll see you day after tomorrow at 0800 hours sharp. But be absolutely sure that you have no seminal emissions before then."

I pulled on my tunic. It was almost impossible to close the front over this roaring erection. The skin was inflamed and hypersensitive. My balls seemed to reverberate as they bounced against my thighs. Each step was torture.

I turned as I reached the door. "Dr. Sax, how many aliens will I meet?"

His expression was enigmatic. "Just one. But that is the equivalent of meeting all of them. Good day, Mr. Stout."

I walked slowly, painfully back to the cubicle, my genitalia swinging and resounding like sledgehammer blows to the groin. I was hornier than a hippo in heavy heat. My head was swimming with a peculiar mixture of fear and anticipation. I couldn't bear the fiery sensations radiating from my cock and nuts, so I swallowed the pink powder Dr. Sax had given me and fell into my bunk. As I dozed off I glanced at the clock: 1200 hours, a very early bedtime.

DAY TWENTY

My head was clear when I awoke. Somebody was at the door of my cube.

"Enter," I yawned. The door slid open. It was Bron. I lay naked on the bunk. He stared at my crotch in amazement. "Moon in Uranus!" he gasped in disbelief. I looked down with sleepy eyes, then jumped up to confront my image in the mirror. An incredible change had occurred while I slept. Dr. Sax's hormone injections had done their biochemical magic—my cock and balls were breathtakingly huge!

How huge? I handled them gingerly at first, then with increasing delight. As I could not believe my eyes, my fingers supplied the proof that this amazing change was real and probably permanent. My gonads were the size of fresh peaches, loaded with nature's juices and swinging freely halfway to my knees. My prick hung down soft and flaccid, but it was already the size of Menelik's impressive sex tool—and I had been on Xenobia for only twenty days! I hefted it in my right hand, bouncing it up and down in my palm like a butcher about to put a salami on the scale. How much bigger would it grow when it was in a state of excitement?

I didn't have to wait long to find out. Bron came up behind me and put his arms around my chest. He looked at me in the mirror. I could feel his magnificent body rubbing against my backside, his stiffening man meat knocking against my ass. I was hotter than a fusion reactor. My hormoned sausage stood at attention, pounding against my abdomen, well above my navel. He reached down and closed his big fist around my love spout. "What happened?"

"It's the hormones, I guess." I didn't have to lie.

"No unauthorized orgasms!" squealed the Guardian Angel. "No unauthorized orgasms!" I flipped a spare tunic over its hovering body, thrusting it into darkness.

Bron smiled at me affectionately. "I'm through worrying about Moira," he told me. "She's made her decision. From now on it's you and me, Antony." He grabbed me again from the rear and kissed the back of my neck. His donkey dong throbbed against my anus. I looked at the clock. It was 0700 hours, but it was the wrong day! I had slept for forty-three hours while the hormones (and the pink powder) were at work! I was due to meet the alien in only an hour!

I struggled away from Bron's embrace. He grabbed me from the front and pressed his strong lips against my mouth, his hands groping at my anus. I wanted to fall back on the bunk and be raped by the beautiful white pile driver, but I knew I couldn't let it happen. Not now. I pushed the man I loved away from me again.

"I have to go now, Bron." His face looked as though I had struck him full force. He stared in disbelief. How could I tell him that I had a meeting with a Vronk? I had pledged secrecy to Dr. Sax. I could not risk seminal emission under any circumstances.

"There's someone else, isn't there?" he demanded, his face red with anger. "It's that bastard in the next cube, isn't it? I heard some talk in the restaurant. One of the spermstuds said he saw you coming out of Menelik's cubicle, and then you had to go to the shower stalls to wash the come off your body. He's the one who taught you the trick about covering the Guardian Angels, isn't he?"

Bron's huge hands doubled into fists. "What is it, Antony?" he shouted. "My cock is twice as big as Menelik's." His lips pulled back in a sneer. "He's nothing but a tired old space fag. And you're no better—talking about love!" His fist swung out and struck me on the side of my head. I fell back on the bunk, stunned. I heard the door slide shut as he stalked out into the hallway.

I rested for a few minutes without moving. Then I walked to the shower stalls. Several spermstuds stared in disbelief at my huge, sperm-swollen nuts as I refreshed myself under the jets of steaming water. The mirror revealed only a minor discoloration where Bron's fist had connected with my temple. I put all thoughts of the future from my head. Perhaps I would be able to convince Bron of my sincerity tomorrow, when his anger had cooled. For now I had to concentrate my mental energy on my upcoming meeting with the Vronk. I took the pneumolift up to Level 1 and tapped on the door marked z.

"Enter," Zschado's gruff voice boomed. He was seated behind his steel desk, his oily black hair and beard glistening in the soft light. His face revealed an expression of vague amusement as he looked me up and down. "Well, 677, you're a bit early. Sit down—please." I sat in the extra pneumochair, my heart pounding in anticipation.

"There is no way to prepare you for what you are about to experience," he said. He nodded to the closed door in the back wall. "In a few minutes a Vronk will come through that door. The only advice I can give you is to be surprised at nothing—and have courage." He rose from his chair with an expression that was unexpectedly sympathetic. As he passed out the door and into the corridor, he whispered, "Good luck!"

I was alone. I waited.

It seemed like hours. I got up and paced the room. Then I sat down again. My heart thudded against my ribs. My head felt light and dizzy. My sperm-filled testicles throbbed and tingled. Suddenly, without warning, the interior door slid open, and the alien entered the room. It was exactly 0800 hours.

"Mizzter Zztout." The alien's voice buzzed with a peculiar metallic sound. "Zzo pleazzed to meet you." I gaped in amazement at the sight before me. My knees felt weak. I had to suppress an almost irresistible urge to laugh hysterically. I rose cautiously from the pneumochair.

How can I describe the physical appearance of this creature? I can compare it, perhaps, to the aardvark native to our Earth, but the Vronk was about as tall as an average human being. It had four limbs, but they were of such strange configuration that comparisons with familiar life-forms don't suffice. It had small forearms ending in four slender, tentaclelike "fingers"; powerful hind legs, upon which it walked, or rather glided, upright and grace-fully; two golden eyes, soft and kind and glowing with intelli-gence; and a mouth and nose combined into one organ, a long, slender, pink-veined proboscis emerging from the rounded form of the head. Two strange organs of unknown purpose bulged from either side of the proboscis, giving the effect of a bizarre trio of genitalia in the middle of the face. Two tiny pointed ears were situated well back on the side of the skull, if indeed normal bone lay beneath. The whole body was covered with a deep mossy green fur, almost as soft as goose down. The fur gleamed and stirred lightly in the softly moving air from the ventilators. The Vronk spoke again.

"You have many quezztionzz, yezz?" The soft golden eyes gazed into mine. My mind was buzzing, but I suddenly felt relaxed and safe.

"What do you do with human sperm?" I asked. It was the first question that came to mind.

"We zztudy it," the Vronk replied. "It givezz uzz knowledge of the univerzze."

"Do you analyze it in a biochemical laboratory?"

"We, our own bodiezz, are the biochemical laboratory." With its tentacle-fingers it indicated the two bulging organs on either side of the proboscis. "Here. We analyzze directly, by ingezzting. Our evolution hazz favored our zzpezziezz with direct chemical exzz-perienzze. We learn from the pure and zzimple zztructure of the DNA code. It izz our food, our drug, our perfume, our zzex, and our enzzyclopedia. We do not need it to zzurvive, but we find it to be an aezzthetic exzzperienzze. It givezz uzz a zzatizzfaction that you would find difficult to conzzieve. Imagine a human being lizzening to beautiful muzzic, having zzex, eating delizziouzz tid-bitzz, and learning about creation all at the zzame time."

We were silent for a moment while I stared into the Vronk's golden eyes in wonder.

"Do not be too flattered, Mizzter Zztout. Yourzz izz not the only zzpezziezz whozze zzperm we collect. It izz, however, among the mozzt interezzting and intriguing."

"But why me?" I asked the Vronk. "Why did you want to meet me face-to-face?"

"Yezz…" the alien mused. "Thizz will be perhapzz difficult for you to underzztand. I wizzh to exzztract the zzperm directly from your tezzticlezz. You, Mizzter Zztout, will have the honor of being the firzzt and perhapzz the only human to have thizz zzexual contact with an alien zzpezziezz. When we heard of your azztounding zzperm production, we dezzided that you would be the outzztanding choizze for the contact."

My mind felt far away, as if it were lost in the vast reaches of the universe, as I pondered the alien's words. The buzzing voice continued.

"Ourzz izz a collective zzpezziezz, Mizzter Zztout. We are not individualzz azz you underzztand the term. We zzhare one mind. We have no individual namezz. We act together, with the knowledge of all of uzz. Thuzz, you will, by your contact with me, be contacting all of the Vronk. Come here to me, Mizzter Zztout."

I felt no fear as I approached the Vronk. I stood stock-still before the intelligent gaze of those golden eyes. The slender fingerlets loosened my tunic, which fell around my ankles. It passed its tiny forearms lightly over the front of my body. The soft, downy fur tickled my skin. My penis began to swell.

"Ah, yezz, your penizz becomezz ready," the Vronk said. "You antizzipate our union."

The alien bent down. Its proboscis approached the tip of my penis. "Are you male or female?" I asked.

"Neither, Mizzter Zztout. And both. All of uzz, I am." The soft, warm tip of the proboscis was like a tiny mouth. It began to envelop the head of my stiffening cock, and I felt a light suction as the alien organ expanded outward to slide over the first few inches of my penis like a thick casing over a sausage. When half the length of my organ had disappeared within this tube of alien flesh, I began to see, or rather feel, pictures in my mind.

The Vronk had established telepathic contact through this touching of the organs. I saw flashes of the Vronk's home planet, an Earthlike globe circling a bright star. I saw their cities—like huge towering termite nests, but all of shining gold, like cathedrals. They were miles tall and laced with passageways and chambers. I saw the spacecraft in which they traveled...their libraries with books of crystal and quartz...their collective telepathic entertainments...floods of images. But superimposed on these was a primary image in which I could see the inside of my own genitalia.

Now I saw—and felt—the wondrous sensations of the alien's tiny tentacular tongue, slimy with alien "saliva," as it began to worm its way into my urethra. A pulsing suction began as the exterior proboscis and the interior tongue slid further down on my throbbing organ. The telepathic image in my mind was that of a tiny eye looking out from the tip of the alien tongue. I saw the inside of my own cock, glowing with reddish capillaries and tingling with nerve endings. I began to moan in delight, and the moaning was accompanied by a rhythmic buzzing sound from deep within the Vronk's chest cavity.

Slowly, gently, almost imperceptibly, the Vronk's biochemical organ slid down the rigid shaft of my prick, slimy and almost hot where the alien and human flesh slid together. My sensual overload was so complete that it was a surprise when I realized that my knees had buckled and that the Vronk was holding me up by my armpits. It was very strong, but gentle. My entire body hung limp in its powerful grip. I relaxed completely, closed my eyes, and gave in to the alien's ministrations.

I concentrated on the telepathic visions. The planetary scenes faded away, and now my consciousness was literally inside my own sex organs. I saw the inside of my cock as a vast cavernous underground passage suffused with reddish light. The alien tongue was an enormous serpent, miles long, with a tremendous girth that slowly worked its way into the mine. Yes, the image was that of a mine shaft, and at the end of it lay a fabulous treasure. The serpent seemed covered with tiny golden scales that glittered in the rosy light. The shaft was barely large enough to admit the serpent's body, which rubbed against the corrugated red walls. Where it rubbed, the mine shaft walls gave off sparks of blue electricity, which sent shivers through my entire body. The serpent had one golden eye in the center of its head. Its tongue flicked in and out, and the center of the tongue contained a tiny sucking mouth. It moved in peristaltic waves deeper and deeper into the mine shaft, my urethra.

The alien organ had reached the base of my cock, both outside and inside. The external proboscis continued its sucking movements, but within the urethra the serpent-tongue slid effortlessly on. The passage gradually narrowed, and the walls were now a lighter color. The serpent's gleaming golden eye was like a searchlight as it plowed deeper and deeper into the restricted passageway, inexorably seeking its goal. Moving under the bladder, it finally wound its way into the vas deferens. Now the walls of the passage expanded outward again and gleamed white and shiny and moist. Sparks of electricity flashed from the serpent's scales. It plunged downward as if into a deep well. Far below I could see a bright red glow: my gonads hanging in their sac! Millions of tiny musical voices sang out ever more clearly as the serpent's head plunged down into the red light. They were the sounds of a multitude of spermatozoa, each singing a tiny song of hopeful life and love.

The passageway opened into a labyrinth of channels, too many to count. The golden serpent shot out its own long tongue and called in a strange, bewitching voice. A myriad little white birds came flying out of the seminal tubules. They wriggled as they flew—or did they swim in a colorless ether? Countless numbers of them flew into the mouth of the serpent. Why did my sperm look like white birds in the telepathic vision? They sang as they flew into the serpent's mouth, until, when it seemed like hours later, they had all disappeared into the body of the serpent. The song slowly died away. The vision was strange and beautiful, and I was dimly aware that tears were running down my cheeks. In fact, my body was racked with shudders and sobs.

Now the serpent-tongue began to withdraw: back up the vas deferens, under the bladder, past the prostate and seminal vesicle, and into the larger passage of the urethra. It paused again at the base of my throbbing penis. Suddenly the telepathic vision reversed, and I was in the body of the Vronk.

I again both saw and felt the inside of the alien's biochemical organs, which bulged out on either side of its proboscis. The interior was like a vast library, with hexagonal niches in the walls stretching out for miles and miles. The walls were white and glittered like soapstone. My sperm-birds flew in by the millions, each singing a different song. Each landed in a separate niche on the wall and began to write its story on the surface within the niche. The stories were told in colored shapes and symbols and mathematical signs, which the tiny creatures painted with their heads, manipulating them like a muralist uses a brush. As they painted their stories, they gradually used up their bodies, until nothing was left but their murals. The murals would last forever, I understood—or at least until the last Vronk passed away—because their collective memory would contain this event perpetually.

I became aware again that I was weeping. Suddenly the Vronk released my spent body, and I fell to my knees, my head touching the floor, gasps and sobs shuddering through my frame. After a few moments, the alien touched my shoulder gently. I raised my head and looked into the infinite golden eyes.

"My zzinzzere thankzz, Mizzter Antony Zztout," the Vronk said. "Pleazze take thizz gift with my gratitude." It pressed a small, flat metallic object into my hand. Then it glided back through the doorway into the secret bowels of Xenobia. I wept again.

Finally I had the courage to look at the clock. It read 0805! This astounding vision of microcosmic infinite sexual contact had taken place in about three minutes! I staggered to my feet, slipped on my tunic, and stumbled out the door into the corridor. Zschado was leaning against the wall with his arms folded across his massive chest.

He smiled sardonically. "Well?" he asked.

He pulled a look of surprise as I ignored him and made my way back to the pneumolift. Exhausted, I rode back up to Level

6 in a daze. The Vronk had drained my testicles completely; they felt positively light, though they still looked huge. I was mentally drained as well. I stood under the jets of hot water in the shower stall for what seemed like forever. I was still on Vronk time. I dried under the air jets and slowly walked back to my cubicle.

As I took off my tunic, I felt a metal object in the pocket. It was the gift the Vronk had given to me. In my light-headed state, I had forgotten it. On closer examination it proved to be a decoder, similar to the ones we had used in survey work. I wondered why the alien had given it to me and what I was supposed to do with it.

The answer arrived several hours later, when a Guardian Angel delivered an ethernote to my cube. It was in mathematical code. I punched the cipher into the decoder. The message read: TO MR. STOUT, WHEN WILL WE SEE YOU AGAIN? SIGNED, V.

DAY TWENTY-FOUR

I awoke with a raging hard-on. Although I had been on the extractor machine for my eighth session only the day before, the hormones had renewed my sex drive overnight, and I was as horny as a mountain goat—with an appetite to match.

It was a "free" day for me—as free as one could be in the completely controlled climate of Xenobia. I slipped on my tunic and boots and headed for the showers. As I stood under the tingling spray, my thoughts wandered. I tried to peer into my uncertain future. My feelings for Bron hadn't changed. For the first time in my life, I was truly in love, but unexpectedly, it was with another man. How could I convince Bron of my sincerity? How could I explain away the misunderstanding that had separated us? My fear of rejection had prevented me from coming to terms with this problem.

As I stood drying under the air jets, I became aware through my reverie that I was being watched. My thoughts of Bron and the warm air had produced another massive erection, and several spermstuds were ogling my huge, throbbing sex tool. Among them was Menelik. He winked at me and drew closer.

"Hey, cutie," he whispered. "You been rehung!" He looked down between my legs with a knowing smile. "Come on over to my cube afterward so I can get a closer look." He had not seen my newly huge cock and balls since Dr. Sax's direct hormone injections had worked their magic.

I couldn't resist Menelik's offer. After breakfast I found myself walking over to his room. The door slid open, and Menelik jumped up from his bunk. He took off his tunic and threw it over the Guardian Angel. He was hot and ready for action, his big dong swelled and throbbing. He pulled my tunic off my body and gazed down hungrily at my already erect cock, at the big, peach-size nuts bouncing against my thighs. He licked his lips.

"What happened to you?" he asked in amazement. "You're hung bigger'n me, and you've been here only three weeks!"

"Dr. Sax did it," I replied. I didn't have time to explain how before Menelik fell to his knees worshipfully. He grabbed my big testicles in both hands and began to knead them while he started to kiss and lick the underside of my rigid pole. "That's right," I ordered. "Suck it real good, Menelik, suck it real good. My cock needs a good working-over."

He grasped the base of my prick with his right hand and pulled it down to attempt get his lips around the engorged head. It was more than a mouthful, almost more than an experienced space fag like Menelik could handle. He gasped and groaned as his distended jaws finally opened wide enough to admit the glans and part of the shaft. He pulled at my big bull balls with his left hand while his right hand slid up and down the rest of my rigid tool. He sucked hungrily, making slurping sounds, his saliva dropping to the floor in puddles.

I needed to get my man meat deeper down Menelik's throat. I grabbed the back of his hairless skull and forced it down on the shaft, obviously beyond the point of comfort. I realized that I wanted to dominate Menelik as he had dominated me during our first encounter. He had revealed to me my true sexual nature. Now I wanted to pay him back in spades!

My hands pushed Menelik's face farther and farther down on the rigid shaft of my thick prick until he began to gag. I was relentless. I teasingly withdrew and then forced it down again. He gagged again and again as I plunged deeper and deeper. His mouth filled with vomit, and I fucked the vomit-filled throat. He fell back, letting a puddle of upchuck fall to the floor.

"Wow, cutie," he gasped, coughing. "You sure are hot this morning. I need my bung hole plugged real bad. OK?" He crawled over to the bunk and lay facedown, spreading his muscular legs and moving his pelvis up and down invitingly. "Come on, baby, ride my ass," he breathed heavily.

I stood over him and looked down at the hairless coppery skin of his buns, which cradled the pink portal of his hot honeypot.

My ramrod, slimy with saliva and vomit, stood ready to invade this puckered paradise.

"Don't make me wait, baby," Menelik moaned. "I ain't had my ass fucked good in a long time." His hole twitched in anticipation. His legs spread wider. His breath came hot and heavy. "Please, baby, please! Fuck me!"

I placed the head of my slimy pile driver against the wrinkled lips of his sphincter. "Ready?" I asked.

"Yeah, cutie, let me have it!" he groaned. I shoved it in ruthlessly, all but the last few centimeters.

"Aie-e-e!" he screamed. His asshole was nice and tight. I guess it was true—he hadn't been fucked in a while.

"Good thing the Guardian Angels don't mind people screaming," I murmured as I withdrew completely. I placed the tip of my cock against his sphincter again. "More?" I asked. "Menelik wants more?" My nuts were aflame with come lust.

It took him a few moments to recover his voice. "Please, baby, please, shove it in my hole again," he moaned in supplication. I waited awhile, teasing his bung hole by rubbing the hot cock head against its now-wet surface. Menelik was gasping in anticipation. "Don't make me wait, baby! Fuck my ass! Hard! Please!" I obeyed and plunged my slimy dick down into the depths of his entrails in one relentless thrust. It went almost all the way in, about two thirds of its new length.

"A-a-arrgghhh!" Menelik's stocky body writhed in ecstasy, his anal canal pulsating against my plunging prick. *"A-a-arrgghhh!"* he groaned again as I forced another couple of centimeters deeper into his straining orifice. Menelik reached back with his left hand and grasped the unused base of my cock. He felt up and down, as if testing the extra portion. "Let me have it all, Antony," he begged. "I think I can take it. Shove it in, stud!"

Something in Menelik's guts was resisting the penetration of the last few centimeters of my supercock, so I fell on him with all my weight and finally drove it home. My pelvis pounded against his heaving buttocks. He screamed in agony and ecstasy at this invasion of his previously unexplored rectal territory.

I fucked his ass without mercy; I wanted to repay him for his previous favors. *Take that!* I thought as I pounded his guts with my butt banger. *That's for making me aware of my sexuality.* I slammed my meat into his hole ruthlessly. *Take that for curing me of the sperm hunger.* I rode his ass like a cowboy on a colt, each heavy slam of my pile driver into his entrails forcing a gasp of breath from Menelik's lungs. Again and again I drove my penetrator deep into his guts.

I looked down at Menelik's muscular body writhing on the bunk beneath the onslaught of my ruthless fuck pole. His copper-color skin gleamed with droplets of sweat. His spine contorted up and down in waves. Soon his pelvis rose up to meet each powerful thrust of my rod, effectively doubling the slamming action to his guts. He groaned again and again in rhythm with my cock slamming into his juicy bung hole.

How could his guts withstand the mauling they were taking? I fucked his ass furiously for almost an hour, carefully withholding my climax until I could stand it no more. The bunk was slimy with his ass juice that was running down his butt cheeks and legs. My swollen bull nuts slapped against the insides of his thighs, and they too were coated with sticky bung juice. I knew that the end of our marathon fuckfest was near when Menelik pleaded in a small voice, "Please, no more, I can't take any more. Please."

I had been holding back, but this was my signal for a triumphant fireworks display. The unruly Menelik had been broken by superior fuckpower. "Mercy," he gasped. "No more, please. Mercy!" My egg sac started to tighten, and I felt a gush of hot seed rush up the length of my red-hot come spout.

He screamed as he felt the scalding custard spray his intestines. The hormone-laced semen burst out in shot after shot. I knew that my heavy grinding of his pelvis against the bunk was stimulating Menelik's rigid prick beyond endurance and that his groans signaled that his own overladen nuts were also releasing their cargo of hot semen in timed rhythm with my own sperm blasts. After agonizing minutes of this final fuck frenzy, my nuts were drained. I pulled out my throbbing seed shooter and stood up shakily.

Menelik lay prone on the bunk as if dead. Finally he breathed deeply and whispered, "*Whee-e-e-e!*"

"I need a shower, Menelik." My body was covered with sweat and sticky with various body secretions from the waist down. For some reason I was thinking of Bron. I was thinking that it was me on the bunk with my ass in the air and Bron doing the butt ramming.

"Go ahead and shower," Menelik sighed. "I'll see you there in a few minutes. I need a bit to recover." He turned over lazily and smiled up at me. His belly was coated with bung juice and come. He looked like a puppy after a full meal. I slipped on my tunic loosely and made for the showers. I felt pleasantly exhausted under the hot sprays and the warm air-jet dryers.

As I exited the shower room, two Guardian Angels were waiting. They grabbed my arms. "Come with us now," they chimed in unison as they forced me into the pneumolift. I knew better than to resist—their antigrav power units were stronger than any human muscle, hormones notwithstanding. I was pretty certain where they were taking me, so I was not surprised when we stopped in front of the door marked z.

The door opened, and Zschado stood up behind his steel desk, glaring at me through his right eye, his enigmatic left eye concealed behind the black eye patch. The robots pushed me inside. The door slid closed, and we were alone. His body-armor links clinked faintly as he moved toward me. *Only a dangerous man needs to wear armored clothing,* I thought. Fear and disgust filled my mind as he stood so close that I could smell his hot, sour breath on my face.

"You've disobeyed the rules of your contract, Spermstud 677," he growled. "I know that you have engaged in unauthorized sperm emissions with Menelik. Don't look surprised. I placed a telebug in Menelik's cubicle, and I heard the sounds of your lust over the past hour." Unexpectedly the scowl on his swarthy face softened. Without warning, he encircled my waist with his big, muscular arms and pulled my body to his. I felt the hard links of the armor biting into my flesh. His towering frame pressed hard against me as he put his fleshy lips to my ear.

"Do not resist me, Antony Stout," he whispered menacingly. "No one can resist Zschado." I could feel his huge erection pressing against my abdomen. I tried to struggle away from this obscene embrace, but Zschado held me fast.

"I've had my eye on you ever since your first day on Xenobia," he continued, now rubbing his groin against my belly. "You are the type of young man I find hard to resist. I can forgive your transgressions. Come and be my consort and rule Xenobia with me." His wiry beard scraped against my neck.

"Think of what I can offer to you," he went on, breathing hard with his disgusting passion. "Wealth beyond measure, the freedom to go anywhere in the known universe, the pleasure of power over other men—and *this*." He grasped my wrist and placed my hand on his crotch, where I felt through the metallic fabric a mammoth, pulsing organ. "We can start with a kiss to seal our bargain…"

He loosened his grasp momentarily, and I sprang away from him, backing up until I was against the wall. "You disgust me, Zschado," I spat. "You know nothing of love. You love only power and the wealth you buy with the sperm of other men. I can never submit to you. Never!"

His expression grew frightful: His lips drew back in a snarl, and his good eye narrowed, flashing with steely determination. "Very well, Antony Stout," he growled through clenched teeth. "Perhaps a little vacation in the solitary dungeons of Xenobia will cause you to reconsider your hasty words."

He pushed a button on the desk console. The inner doorway to the secret precincts of Xenobia opened, and Baker and Charlie floated into the office. "Escort Spermstud 677 to the solitary cell called Purgatory, where he can contemplate his sins." The Guardian Angels grasped my arms and pushed me into the dim interior passageway. As the door slid shut, I heard Zschado's voice: "Goodbye, Antony, my dearest. Until we meet again…"

Tears of fear and rage blurred my vision as the robots pulled me down spiral staircases, across long steel ramps, and past innumerable doorways and blind passages. I caught glimpses of cell doors with tiny windows at eye level. Sometimes I heard muffled groans from behind the doors. I saw refrigerated chambers with thousands of vials of sperm arranged and labeled on metal racks. Strange smells and weird flashes of colored light penetrated the gloom.

The Guardian Angels forced me ever onward until we finally stopped before an anonymous doorway. As it opened, the robots pushed me inside. The heavy armored door slid shut with a pneumatic hiss and a metallic clang. Then silence, absolute silence. I was imprisoned in Zschado's Purgatory. How many innocents like me suffered in the depths of Xenobia?

As my eyes became accustomed to the gloom, I explored my solitary cell. It was completely padded with black plastoid—floor, walls, and ceiling. Otherwise, the cell had only two features: a small recessed light, out of reach in the high ceiling, and a smooth body-waste trough on the wall opposite the entrance. This was all, except for a sliding panel in the door.

I sank to the floor, shaking with anger and terror. Soon I fell into a deep slumber filled with nightmares. When I awoke I found a tray of food and drink on the floor beneath the sliding panel in the door. I ate ravenously, then slept again.

There was no accurate way to keep track of time in my new quarters. I tried placing my veloid boots on the floor in a pattern, starting with the corner of the cell to the right of the door. I moved one boot every time a tray of food appeared through the sliding panel. Unfortunately, I had no way of knowing if the meals came on any kind of regular schedule. I never felt hungry, though. Zschado obviously wanted me to stay healthy, at least physically.

As time crawled by I sank into lethargy and slept, dreaming of freedom. I dreamed I was back on my little survey ship, cruising through the star-filled blackness of space. I dreamed of my beloved Bron, his big muscular body pressed against mine; his pale, marble manhood standing huge and erect away from his gleaming thighs; his silvery hair shining.

I awoke with a towering hard-on. Bron's voice seemed to be whispering in my ear. "I love you, Antony," he was saying. "Stroke your beautiful dick for me." My hands moved downward on my supine body, stroking my belly and my thighs as if controlled by another mind. The position of the boots showed that twenty-seven meal trays had come and gone. I was long overdue for a nut flushing. My cock throbbed painfully, and my near-to-bursting testicles yearned for release.

I watched my big pulsing dick in the gloomy light of Purgatory. I grasped my scrotum with my left hand and massaged my swollen gonads, pulling them down and away from my body as I had learned to enjoy on the extractors. The soft voice seemed to whisper in my head: "Beat that big beautiful meat for me, Antony. Beat it hard!" I pictured Bron's handsome face smiling down at me.

I spit saliva into my right hand and began to slide it up and down the long cock shaft. "That's right, Antony, beat that man meat for me," Bron's voice continued, urging me on. "Let me see it shoot a big load of sperm!" I doubled the speed of my stroking fist. Soon I was pounding my meat mercilessly as the voice continued its cajoling: "Beat it hard! Beat it real hard, Antony!" I pulled and twisted my heavy nuts in a frenzy of self-love. My big meaty man pole gave off slapping sounds as my fist pounded it into submission.

My semen-filled balls twitched and heaved as they began to release their bounty of male milk. It gushed in torrid spurts up the length of my tortured come spout, spraying over my belly in big white gobs. "That's it, Antony, show me your man juice," the voice moaned. "Let it go!" Load after load of hot, steaming come spattered my chin, my chest, my belly, and finally my wrists as my pelvis strained upward in the throes of orgasm. I pulled and pounded on my pulsating prick, determined to flush every last drop from my contracting balls. I moaned with the intensity of the orgasm.

As the last drops of white cream ran down my arm, I heard the voice again. "Har, har, har!" it laughed mischievously. "You sure are a good sperm producer!"

I sprang to my feet. "Zschado!" I cried. "You bastard!" He had been watching me all along while I beat my meat!

"You're right, my dearest, I am a bastard," he replied. "My mother was a whore on Mars colony, and my father was most likely a space pirate, like me. I owe my existence to a defective contraseed pill. Lady Luck has been with me ever since." Zschado's voice guffawed again. "Do you realize how much the sperm on your belly is worth?" he asked.

"Fuck you, Zschado!" I screamed at the disguised telebug in the ceiling. "Fuck you and your mother!"

"Sleep well, my darling. Sleep well..." the voice faded away.

And I did sleep again. I was exhausted from the orgasm and then from my rage at Zschado. I cried in frustration as I drifted off to dreams of freedom. It seemed like only moments later when a voice whispered in my ear, "Antony! Wake up!"

"You bastard," I gurgled, still half asleep. But it wasn't Zschado's gruff voice I was hearing. "Bron?"

"No cutie, it's me—Menelik. Don't talk too loud."

"Menelik! How—?"

"Shhh! Let me explain. I'm going to get you out of here."

"How did you find me?" I whispered.

"I was in the corridor outside the showers when I saw Zschado's Angels grab you. Then, that night, when I was asleep, I heard a buzzing voice in my head. It told me everything that had happened to you."

The Vronk! I thought. They had been in constant telepathic contact with my thoughts since our merging.

"I knew you were friendly with Bron the Lunarian, because I saw you together in the restaurant so often," Menelik continued. "Bron and I talked the next morning. He had heard the same voice, and he knew what I knew. We put our heads together and figured out a plan to get you both completely free of Xenobia. I bribed the librarian to get the secret diagrams of the inside passageways of Xenobia. I got here by crawling through a ventilation shaft on the seventh level. The cell door is easy to open from the outside with a magkey."

He pulled me to my feet. "Wow, you need a shower!" he said, sniffing. He handed me a clean tunic.

"I also found out about Zschado's sleep schedule," he added. "We have two hours to get you cleaned up and away from Xenobia before he wakes up. Bron is going with you. He understands and forgives everything. I explained to him that you came to my cubicle just for sex—because you had the sperm hunger, that's all. Your scout ship is fueled and stocked and ready to blast off. The guy who manages the cargo bay where your ship is stored is a fuck buddy of mine." Menelik's smile flashed in the dim light of Purgatory.

"Zschado doesn't know the half of what happens on Xenobia," Menelik leered. "Most everyone hates his guts and can't resist the opportunity to fuck up his plans. So we got plenty of cooperation, cutie."

He grabbed my arm and pulled me out into the dim passageway. Straight ahead I saw an open grating in the wall. Menelik pushed me inside. It was just big enough to crawl through on my hands and knees. I heard a soft rasp of metal as Menelik pulled the grating shut behind him. We were crawling through the solid basalt core of Xenobia. Not far ahead a soft light shone through a grating on the other end of the shaft, twenty meters of solid rock shaped by laser blasters.

I pushed open the grating, and we stepped out into the corridor on Level 7, the deepest on the planetoid. The hallway was deserted, as was the shower room in which I washed the crud from my body.

"How long was I in Purgatory?" I asked Menelik as I dried under the air jets.

"Almost two weeks," he answered, shaking his head apologetically. "It took us that long just to lay the bribes and make our plans. We had to interrupt our actions every three days for our stints on the extractors. Everything had to appear normal and aboveboard. We were very careful. Now, quick, up to Bron's cube. He's waiting for you."

We hurried through the deserted corridor and took the pneumolift to Level 6. They had planned carefully: It was the middle of the night shift according to Xenobia's artificial clocks, and all seemed deserted. Behind the closed doors of the extractor rooms, I could picture dozens of spermstuds being juiced, their bodies trapped in suspended orgasm.

We quietly hurried to Bron's cubicle. The door opened, and Bron stopped pacing the floor and rushed over to me. He stared into my eyes silently for a few moments, then he put his arms around me tenderly and pressed me to his beautiful body. Both our cocks began to stiffen beneath our tunics.

"Don't take too long with the lovey-dovey stuff, studs," said Menelik. "I'll be in Cargo Bay 16 getting your ship ready." We heard the door slide open and shut. Bron pressed his warm lips to mine. His tongue slid into my mouth, and his big hands rubbed my back and buttocks. His pelvis thrust into mine, grinding his rigid man pole against my stomach. "Antony, Antony," he whispered passionately. "I never want to lose you again."

We were lost in each other's bodies, so much so that we hardly noticed when the door slid open again. *Was Menelik back already?* I thought.

We turned to see—Zschado!

He loomed in the doorway like a ghastly apparition from a nightmare. His one good eye gleamed red with malice, and his massive left fist clenched and unclenched furiously at his side. "So!" he roared. "The lovers try to escape the wrath of Zschado!" His right hand was concealed behind his back.

He moved toward us slowly and deliberately. His right hand appeared from behind his back holding a strange yet somehow familiar object.

"Look out, Antony!" Bron screamed frantically. "He's got a weirding stick!"

A crystalline wand flashed in Zschado's fist. Now I remembered! The weirding stick had been outlawed on all civilized worlds for over a hundred years. It had been used for torture and interrogation during the Psychwars. The fiendish device put the receiver into a kind of cataleptic trance, subject to the will of the holder. The only functions left operating were sight and speech, so that interrogation could proceed unhampered. I had seen the weapon in the Council's academy training manuals.

But before we could make any move, Zschado touched Bron's forehead with the weirding stick. Bron gasped and fell over backward. He lay helpless on the floor, his eyes locked on my confrontation with this pirate-devil. His body was frozen, but he could still speak. "Fight him, Antony!" he yelled.

It was no use. Zschado was much bigger and stronger than I. He clamped his powerful left hand around my windpipe and waved the weirding stick in front of my face.

"Well, Bron, you see that your lover has no fight in him," Zschado sneered. "Now you will enjoy seeing Zschado possess his pretty young body in a way that will make him my helpless and willing sex slave."

"You bastard!" Bron shouted.

"That's right, I am a bastard. My mother was a whore on Mars colony." He looked out of the corner of his eye at Bron's helpless form lying rigid on the floor. "You ass! Do you think your shouting will prevent me from possessing my little darling Antony right in front of your eyes?" Zschado tightened his grip on my windpipe. His baleful eye riveted my own.

"Perhaps you are wondering why I do not use the weirding stick on your head, my pet," he leered menacingly. "It is because I want you to feel and struggle as I possess you completely, body and soul!" He tightened his viselike grip on my throat. My knees began to go weak with fear and loathing.

He clicked off the weirding stick and thrust it into his belt. His right hand was then free to loosen the magloops on his fly front to reveal his cock. It slithered out of his trousers heavily.

Bron and I gasped in amazement. The thing that revealed itself to our startled eyes was no human organ but a thick, shiny, snakelike machine, covered with thin plates of gleaming, silvery metal. It slithered and hissed, and the metal plates expanded as it began to stand up like a cobra in an attack posture. "Holy Jupiter!" I yelled. "What *is* that thing?"

"Suffering Saturn!" I heard Bron's voice whisper in disbelief. Zschado tightened his grip on my throat and lovingly stroked his strange organ. "It's my Pseudocok!" he said proudly. "My wonderful Pseudocok! My darling Pseudocok! It obeys my every whim. Would you like a demonstration?"

Suddenly the thing shot out lengthwise, its sharp, pointy head poised over Bron's face. It slapped him on the cheek several times, leaving a series of fine abrasions that began to drip blood. "And that's not all!" Zschado announced, lifting a set of plastoid sacs from his trousers—three of them. They hung below the Pseudocok like three artificial testicles.

"You see, I have an unlimited supply of sperm—as much as I could ever use," Zschado boasted. "Before I left my quarters, I filled my seed tanks with three kinds of sperm. Tank one has sperm from Antony, tank two has sperm from Bron, and tank three has sperm from Menelik. So I am prepared for every possible treason." He giggled. "Take a taste of your lover's jism, Bron, dear." The tip of the Pseudocok squirted a generous portion of semen onto Bron's helpless upturned face.

The uncanny sex machine retracted back into itself with a metallic whir. Zschado turned to me. "Take a good look, my dearest," he said as the Pseudocok then lengthened and poised itself a few centimeters in front of my astonished eyes. The head expanded and morphed into a shiny sphere spitting blue sparks of electricity, which zapped my nose. Then the entire shaft expanded outward so that it thickened to the girth of a man's biceps. The metal plates flipped up and down like the wings of a metallic insect.

"You see, my dearest," Zschado gloated, "I can thus possess you completely." The Pseudocok began to slither between my legs and then curve upward as it found its way to my helpless anus. The head was now smooth and pointy and hot as it wormed its way into my sphincter.

"No!" I screamed. "Please, Zschado!"

I saw a long drool of saliva roll down Zschado's chin. "Yes, my little darling, yes. Whatever Zschado wants, Zschado gets." The Pseudocok began to expand outward again, stretching my rectum painfully. Zschado's good eye was rolling back in his head, showing only white. The Pseudocok was forcing its way deeper into my rectum, now burning hot and sending out crackling bolts of electricity.

"You're mad, Zschado!" I gasped. In answer, the Pseudocok began to twist into my entrails like an electronic drill. "No!" I screamed in agony. "No!" A strange yellow foam began to collect at the corners of Zschado's lips. His teeth started to chatter. "Yes, yes, yes, y-y-yesss..."

Suddenly, without warning, the Pseudocok slithered out of my rectum and retracted into Zschado's crotch with a loud clank. His grip on my throat ceased abruptly as he fell sideways to the floor of Bron's cubicle. Little gurgling noises came from his throat, and a trickle of greenish snot issued from his nose. I quickly snatched the weirding stick from Zschado's belt and unweirded Bron. He stood up shakily, wiping the semen from his face with the hem of his tunic as I massaged my sore neck. We stood there, staring down at Zschado. He jerked, then gurgled. His right eyelid slammed open and shut like a broken camera shutter.

"Give me a hand," said Bron. "Let's take him over to Dr. Sax's office."

We grabbed Zschado's ankles and dragged him into the corridor. I pounded on the door marked 666. A sleepy Dr. Sax appeared, rubbing his red goatee. "My word!" he exclaimed at the sight of Zschado's twitching body. "Quick, help me put him into the resuscitation chamber." Now, with three people, we were able to lift Zschado's massive frame into the transparent tube in the next room. Dr. Sax adjusted the life-sign monitors, and soon the pirate's body ceased its jerking and lay still.

"I guess I'll have to reconstruct him completely," Dr. Sax said after he had heard our harrowing story. "After the lower part of his body was crushed in a meteor collision, I fabricated a cyborg set of hips and legs. The sexual functions were another matter. He wasn't satisfied with the more or less human-looking robot penis and testicles with which I equipped him. All the nerve endings were operating satisfactorily, hooked up to the central nervous system network. He could have enjoyed a completely wonderful sex life with one or any number of partners of his choice. But no, not Zschado. He was always obsessed with sexual power. He visited a renegade robot engineer in the sleazy underworld section of Nuevahavana and had himself equipped with that monstrosity with which he invaded Antony's body. Money was no object, since the sperm traffic provided him with unlimited wealth. I warned him that this complicated Pseudocock put him in danger of neural overload. Well, he finally overdid it! Now he must be reconstructed completely." Dr. Sax smiled at Bron and me ruefully. "I probably had better do some additional work on his psyche as well," he added. "He has been a bit much lately. Now, perhaps it is best that you two leave Xenobia for good." He turned to me and patted me on the cheek with his beefy hand. "Yours has certainly been the strangest visit to Xenobia I have ever witnessed, Antony, and I have been here almost from the very beginning and seen many bizarre events."

He fingered his goatee thoughtfully. "Wait here for just a moment." He bustled out into the deserted corridor, to return a few minutes later with two bulging plastoid pouches and a small black box.

"These are the spermstud salaries you have coming to you," he said as he handed a pouch each to Bron and me. "Actually, I doubled the amount to compensate for your pain and terror at the hands of Zschado. The vaults of Xenobia are so full of Vronkian gold that this amount will never be missed." Dr. Sax opened the black box and handed it to me. "These are for you to use wisely," he said. "Twelve vials of pure megahormone extract." He kissed us both on the cheek. "Now, off Xenobia with you both. You have caused enough trouble."

We thanked Dr. Sax and hurried to Cargo Bay 16. "What took you so long?" asked Menelik, who was pacing up and down the shiny floor under my scout ship. Bron and I were impatient to blast off.

"Ask Dr. Sax," I said as I shook Menelik's hand. "He'll fill you in all the details." Bron and I climbed into the hatch of the little spacecraft and shot the bolts. Through the viewport we saw Menelik waving goodbye as he went through the pressure doors and into the interior of the complex. The lights dimmed as the cargo bay depressurized. The gravbeam pushed us out into the starry blackness of space, and we slowly drifted away from the pockmarked face of Xenobia.

We were free.

"Where to?" Bron asked, sitting at the console.

A buzzing voice answered in my mind: "Mizzter Zztout, you muzzt go to Marzz...to Marzz...to Marzz..." The voice faded in mental echoes. The Vronks were listening and watching.

"Mars colony," I answered. "I've never been there"

"Sounds good!" Bron replied cheerfully. "I've never been there either." He punched up the trajectory on the viewscreen. Mars was on the other side of the sun. The trip would take five weeks. Bron set the coordinates on automatic. He rose from the console and took me in his arms. "Now, Antony, as I was saying before we were interrupted by—"

"I never want to hear that name again!" I interjected. "Never!"

Bron took my arm and led me back to the sleeping quarters. He removed the tunic from his big, muscular body. I shed my tunic as well. His huge, beautiful cock was standing firm and erect. He pushed me down on the larger bunk and lay down beside me, pressing his lips against mine, his tongue probing the inner recesses of my mouth, his massive member nudging my side like a freakish fifth limb. I rolled over on my stomach. I was thinking of Menelik's groans as I fucked his ass. Now I needed to feel that way myself.

"Please, Bron," I implored. "Fuck my ass. Fuck it hard and deep and long."

"We've got five weeks," Bron replied softly as he rubbed the tip of his mammoth prick against my sphincter. "Is that long enough?"

"Maybe not," I answered as the darkness of infinite space closed around us.

Dream Studs of Kama Loka

PART ONE

"I suppose you're wondering why I asked you here," said Dr. Wünder.

"Yes, I *was* asking myself that question." Somehow I felt foolish saying that. I looked directly into Dr. Wünder's deep black eyes. The golden light of a late-December sunset filtered through the windows, softly illuminating the crowded bookshelves, piles of journals, and stacks of term papers in Dr. Wünder's office. He picked up a black-bound printout and handed it to me.

"Have you read this, Mr. Hoffman?" he asked.

I looked at the title: "Neurochemistry of Lucid Dreaming—Saratoga University Dream Research Laboratory." I quickly flipped through the report: about forty pages, lots of charts and graphs.

"I've heard about it," I said, "but this is the first time that I've seen a copy of the actual report."

Dr. Wünder passed a hand through his thick salt-and-pepper hair, then smiled, showing a set of strong ivory teeth. He stood and paced the worn carpet for a few moments. I noticed a large bulge through his khaki trousers that indicated that he was not wearing any underwear. I had noticed this succulent swelling before, during various classes of his I had taken during my graduate work at Saratoga University. My mouth watered at the thought of sucking Dr. Wünder's dick someday. He was just my type. He reminded me of my father.

He paused next to the chair in which I was sitting and put his hand on my shoulder. His crotch was right at my eye level. Could he know that I was thinking of putting my lips around his cock? My own dick was beginning to stir. I placed the report on my lap to hide the telltale bulge in my own trousers.

"I'm going to explain briefly," he said, "and then I'm going to offer you a chance at an incredible adventure." He reached down

and picked up the folder from my lap, revealing the obvious outline of my turgid erection. My mouth was dry, and my heartbeat
pounded in my ears. Had he noticed?

Dr. Wünder resumed his chair behind the desk and paged
through the report. "May I call you Ted?" he asked.

"Of course," I answered.

"Well, Ted, you remember my lectures on the neurochemistry
of the dream state?" I nodded. The previous semester I had followed with great interest his descriptions of the research then
being conducted in the Dream Lab.

"Lucid dreaming, as you know, is a special state of REM sleep,"
he continued. "When dreaming occurs, it is invariably accompanied by REM—that is, rapid eye movement. Lucid dreaming is
induced by sending a small electric current into the brain of the
dreamer after the onset of REM to signal him that he is dreaming. Once the dreamer is aware that what he is experiencing is a
dream, then he is free to direct the course of the dream as he
chooses. Are you with me so far?"

"I'm familiar with the theoretical ideas," I answered. "But what
does this have to do with me?"

"The Lucid Dreaming Project that we have just completed
used volunteers such as housewives, blue-collar workers, secre-
taries—the usual suspects. They were paid a small amount to
sleep at the Dream Lab a few times a week and to be interviewed
the next morning by one of the lab technicians. But these volunteers lacked one essential quality: motivation. Or, to put it
more bluntly, desire.

"My colleagues have decided not to continue the Lucid
Dreaming Project for the present," he went on, "at least until certain aspects of our research become clearer. They believe that
there may be a certain danger involved. My position is that we
should proceed at once."

"And me?" I asked.

"You must know that I am an expert at deep character analy-
sis, Ted," he said, staring directly at me with his stern dark eyes.
"I have been observing you in my classes since you entered the

graduate program, and I have decided that you would be an ideal subject to help me with my research. You have strong desires—very strong indeed. You try to hide them, but they are there. You're young and healthy. You have a sense of curiosity and adventure. And you have a quality that is indispensible to me. Your training in the mental sciences has equipped you with an ability to discriminate between one psychological event and another and to be creative with them."

Dr. Wünder went to the window and gazed pensively out across the campus at the golden light of the winter sunset. He continued. "Even though our project has been officially shelved for the time being, we were able to perfect our equipment for future research. I refuse to allow the timidity of my colleagues to hamper the progress of my research."

He paused and turned to face me. Was it my imagination, or did the bulge in his khaki trousers seem larger, as if his cock was semihard?

"The most extraordinary thing we discovered, which is only hinted at in the official report, is that our research subjects seem to have visited the same place in their lucid dreams," he said. "Over sixty percent reported the existence of this locale. It is called Kama Loka, the Dream City of Desire. It is this exciting possibility that I want to explore with your help."

He came over to me and sat on the edge of the desk. As he did so, the fabric of his trousers pulled tight over his cock and balls, revealing their full massive dimensions. He leaned over and put his hands on my shoulders, looking deeply into my eyes. "If you should agree, these further experiments will have to be kept absolutely secret—just between you and me. My colleagues would not approve."

My mouth was dry. I tried not to stare at his distended crotch, which was just two feet away and level with my eyes. "Will you assist me, Ted?" he asked.

I felt a flush of hot blood race from my groin to the top of my head—desire! "Yes," I said, hearing my voice as if from a distance. "Yes, I'll help."

"Good! Excellent! Now, listen closely. At first thought, one might think that the dream world, which you will explore, contains no hard facts and so there is nothing objective. However, a man's character and desires *are* objective in that they exist whether we like them or not. So the dream realm of Kama Loka is subject to laws, but not to the laws of physics. Its laws are more like the laws of psychology.

"Few of us are completely integrated personalities," he continued. "Our daylight desires may appear to be relatively harmonious, but appearances are deceptive. There are unconscious desires conflicting with the neatly organized patterns of conscious life. There are desires that have been forgotten or repressed. In lucid dreaming, if we dislike the image worlds that our memories and desires create for us—if we are horrified by them—we can immediately change them by an effort of the will, even though this may be painful. This is something the ordinary dreamer cannot do. But you will be able to do it with the help of our newly developed equipment.

"You must remember that any personages you may encounter in the lucid dream world have their own kind of reality. They are called revegens, or dream people. Revegens may be personal creations of your own mind, or they may be creatures of the collective unconscious, obeying their own laws. Treat them with respect. Understood?"

"Yes, I understand," I said. "When do we start?"

"Tonight. Immediately!" Dr. Wünder took one last look at the fading coppery sky and pulled the heavy drapes over the window, plunging the office into gloomy shadows. He clicked on a small reading lamp on his desk, then pulled a small metal box from the top drawer. There was stenciling on the lid: PROPERTY OF DREAM RESEARCH LABORATORY—SARATOGA UNIVERSITY. He opened the box and handed it to me. "This is your ticket to Kama Loka—Dream City of Desire."

Inside the box rested what at first glance I took to be a pair of oversize reading glasses. Closer examination revealed something more like welders' goggles, with lightly tinted lenses held by a soft black rubbery frame, securable with an elastic headband. From four small electrodes—one at the corner of each eye and one at each temple—dangled long, thin black wires. At the bottom of the box lay a pair of thin black elastic gloves with similar electrodes and wires at each fingertip and at each knuckle. I looked at Dr. Wünder in puzzlement. He smiled at my bewilderment and explained.

"This equipment was developed in the Dream Research Lab," he said. "The spectacles and gloves enable the researcher to communicate with the dreamer by way of the Lucid Dream Monitor, without waking him or interrupting the dream. When the monitor senses that REM is occurring, it sends a minuscule electrical tingle to the corners of the dreamer's eyes. When the dreamer feels this tiny stimulus, he knows that what he is experiencing is a dream, and then he can begin to direct that dream in a conscious fashion. You with me?"

"Yes," I answered. "I've read about how this would theoretically work."

"It's not just theory anymore. Take my word for it—it works." He pointed to the gloves. "This is the beautiful part. The gloves enable the dreamer to communicate directly with the researcher in real time, while the lucid dream is in progress. You will be lying on your back, with your hands resting on your abdomen. When you want to communicate with the researcher, you simply move your fingers as if you were typing on a standard keyboard. In actuality your fingers won't move, but the electrodes are so sensitive that they pick up faint muscular potentials that occur on the subconscious level, which is where the dreamer is at that moment. The computer in the Lucid Dream Monitor then deciphers the hand movements as if on a keyboard and transcribes them so that they can be read by the researcher. So you can talk to me, but unfortunately, I won't be able to talk to you, except to say yes or no.

"I can send you a signal during your dream through the electrodes in the spectacles. One short electrical tingle at the corners of the eyes means 'yes,' two short tingles mean 'no.' Understood?"

"One short means 'yes,' and two shorts mean 'no,'" I repeated.

"Good, let's get started." He walked over to the divan across the office. "We'll plan for you to sleep here in the office tonight and several more nights this week. This oversize divan is very comfortable, I assure you. Come over here and take off your shoes. And loosen your belt and any restricting clothing." As I followed his instructions, I watched him uncover a small black console on a low table beside the divan. Its front panel was crowded with glowing biographs, control knobs, a small keyboard, a tracking ball, and a monitor.

"Lie back and relax, Ted." Dr. Wünder slipped the soft elastic gloves over my hands, tugging the wristbands until they were snug. Then he slipped the spectacles over my eyes and pulled the elastic band tight around my head.

"Now drink this." He handed me a small glass filled with a pale pink liquid.

"What is it?" I asked with some trepidation.

"It's acetylcholine," he replied. "It stimulates the dream-making chemistry of the brain. Perfectly safe, I assure you."

I downed the chemical in two gulps, then I lay back.

"Comfy?" he queried.

"Yes. OK. No problem."

He slid a small, firm pillow beneath the nape of my neck, then he attached all the electrode wires from the spectacles and gloves to receptacles behind the monitor. He sat on a low chair in front of the device and began to type commands on the keyboard. I took one last furtive glance at Dr. Wünder's crotch, illuminated by the glow of the instrument panel, bulging through the soft khaki fabric. I turned my head and gazed at the ceiling, not feeling the slightest bit sleepy, what with all the excitement.

A soft, continuous low tone began to emanate from the machine. "Your personal dream tone, synthesized by the monitor," said Dr. Wünder. "It will facilitate your dream production."

I felt a small tingle at the corner of each eye. "That's the long REM signal," Dr. Wünder said. "When you feel that, you'll know you're dreaming. Sleep well, Ted, and remember: What's real?"

"OK, Doc. Should we test the gloves too?" I asked.

"Sure, if you like. Go ahead and type a message as if your fingers were on a keyboard." I typed, THE QUICK BROWN FOX JUMPED OVER THE LAZY DOG. The monitor whirred briefly, and I heard the printer click as it printed out my message. Dr. Wünder tore off the top of the paper and walked to the side of the divan. "Sit up, Ted, and look at the message. Read what you sent." I sat up and pulled off the goggles. The message printout read, PLEASE, DR. WÜNDER, MAY I PLAY WITH YOUR BIG FAT DICK?

My face turned beet-red. But I couldn't help staring at the thickening bulge in Dr. Wünder's khakis as he stood towering over me. He said, "Take off the gloves, Ted." I slipped the gloves from my hands and watched in fascination as the fabric-covered prick uncoiled, lengthened, and thickened, moving upward toward his belt as it grew. "Go ahead, boy," he said. "I've been needing a good massage."

I reached up with both hands and began to softly rub his big cock, one hand on the base and the other kneading the swollen head. I pulled it back and forth through the cloth, rubbing the sensitive head against the coarse khaki.

"Can I take it out, please?" I begged.

I looked up into Dr. Wünder's face to find him smiling with pleasure. "Loosen my belt," he commanded. I unhitched his belt and unbuttoned the first button of his pants. As soon as the waistband was released, his thick prick sprang straight up, protruding at least three inches above the tops of his khakis. It rocked back and forth slightly, like a great snake entranced by the charmer's flute.

I grabbed the base of his prick through his trousers, and with the other hand I started kneading the swollen head. A few glistening drops of precome escaped from the orifice.

"Can I lick it, please, Dr. Wünder?"

In response Dr. Wünder put his hands on the back of my head and forced my face against his fleshy dick head. My lips found a dribble of precome and licked it up eagerly, becoming hungry for more-substantial fare.

"That's it, son, lick that big fat dick head!" Dr. Wünder urged. As I licked, the head swelled to such a girth that I wondered whether I could get it into my stretched lips at all.

Just then the door to the office banged open, and a flashlight swept around the darkened room. A loud baritone voice announced, "Security Chief Jenkins!" His boots thudded slowly across the floor as he advanced on the divan, his flashlight trained on my face. The beam picked out Dr. Wünder's huge erect prick twitching above the loose waistband of his khakis, inches from my face. "Wha-a-at have we he-e-ere?" Jenkins boomed in faux shock. Wünder and I froze in consternation.

Jenkins picked up the metal box stenciled PROPERTY OF DREAM RESEARCH LABORATORY. He turned it over and examined it carefully. "University property, missing since yesterday," he said. "This is getting serious."

Jenkins drew his pistol from its holster and began to stroke the tender underside of Dr. Wünder's cock. "My pistol is harder than your pistol," he chortled. "Wait a minute! I've got to get some evidence here." He pulled a tape measure from his uniform pocket.

"Here, hold this for me." He shoved the barrel of the pistol into my mouth. I heard a metallic click. "Safety catch," he explained. "We don't want you to get a mouthful you didn't bargain for." I tasted the cold metallic tang of steel against my tongue, the pistol grip hanging from my mouth. As I watched in fascination, Jenkins unbuttoned the rest of the fly front of Dr. Wünder's khakis. As the trousers slid down to his thighs, Wünder's huge dick sprang out and up to its full unbelievable dimensions. "A right nice-looking pistol you got there, Doc," the security chief said.

Jenkins began to make measurements of the doctor's dick with the tape. He murmured to himself as he made notes in a small notebook. "Seven p.m., December 17. Discovered Wünder being fellated by nerdy grad student. Missing university property in the vicinity. Cock dimensions at full erection being ten and three quarters inches, enough to choke a horse."

He put away the notebook and tape and began to stroke his own crotch through his trousers, where a noticeable bulge was growing. He put one hand on Wünder's dick shaft and began to unzip his own trousers with the other hand. He pulled aside the fly of his underwear and swung out his very large semierect prick. "Think you can handle two of these fuckers, sonny?" he asked. "Oh, I almost forgot." Jenkins eased the pistol from my mouth.

"Try this instead," he teased as he pulled my face into position against his stiffening cock. I sucked the head and as much of the shaft into my mouth as I could handle, but it was growing bigger and thicker by the moment, forcing my jaws apart.

"You're a hungry, growing boy," said Jenkins. "You need more meat!" He pulled Dr. Wünder over to him until they were pressed hip to hip and the doctor's long prick was rubbing against my cheek. "Take 'em both in, boy!"

I opened my jaws as wide as I could and was rewarded with the feeling of the second dick sliding into my hungry mouth. Dribbles of precome ran down my lips as I slurped and sucked on two mighty hunks of meat at once.

"Wait a minute," said Dr. Wünder, "just wait one minute there. You can't force this student to suck two dicks at the same time, just like that!"

"Looks like he wasn't doing such a bad job with just one dick when I walked in here," Jenkins replied. "Well, OK, he don't have to suck two dicks if you say so."

He put the tip of his pistol to the head of Dr. Wünder's prick and pulled the trigger. The head of the doc's dick exploded in a burst of white cream that splattered all over my face and chest. Wünder sank slowly to his knees. "What's real?" he gurgled as he keeled over to one side. His long, shattered dick stalk oozed thick come like a broken milkweed.

"No more Mr. Nice Guy," growled Jenkins. "Now, suck my cock, nerd, and suck it good—or your head'll look worse than the doc's dong." He forced his rock-hard dick between my lips and pressed his pistol to my temple. As his stiff come cannon began to invade the back of my throat, I started to gag. He grabbed me by the hair and pulled my head back. "You ain't no good for a cocksucker," he grunted. "I'm gonna take you to see the Sukmaster. He'll show you how to suck a man's dick, or you'll choke to death tryin'."

Jenkins handcuffed my wrists behind my back and led me out into the chilly night air. He opened the rear door of his security van and pushed me to the floor of the cargo space. He drove like a maniac. I rolled back and forth as he careened around corners on screeching tires. The breakneck night ride was a blur of flashing lights and signs until he finally braked with a squeal of rubber and turned off the engine.

The rear door opened, and Jenkins grabbed me by the collar and pulled me to my feet. I looked up unsteadily and saw a tall red-and-orange neon sign flashing garishly overhead: SUSIE'S TRUCK STOP. Below that glowed a smaller sign in green neon: BLOW JOBS—24 HOURS A DAY.

I remembered the truck stop. When I got horny and bored with my studies, I used to drive out on the old highway to Susie's. The men's rest room had an entrance off the back parking lot. Many a night I sat in the last toilet stall and sucked every juicy dick that presented itself through one of the glory holes. I used to get back home at two or three in the morning after those rampages of cock sucking.

But now there was that new sign: BLOW JOBS—24 HOURS A DAY. I had certainly never noticed *that* before. Now someone was walking toward us across the wet asphalt. I recognized his face: the busboy who cleared the dishes from the tables and booths. He was wearing a fancy cowboy outfit of white kid leather with chrome studs, embroidered with a satiny thread of pink, red, purple, and gold. Instead of the usual motifs of steer heads, though, these designs showed stylized penises in various stages of excitement. His shiny white boots gleamed with red, green, and orange highlights in the neon lights.

"Meet the Sukmaster," said Jenkins.

The Sukmaster looked me up and down and smiled. His mouth was devoid of teeth, showing only soft pink gums and a long red tongue. "So you're the new pussy mouth!" he said. "How much experience have you had? What's your name?"

"I'm Ted, and I don't know what you're talking about," I replied.

"Oh, come on, gimme a break!" He grabbed my jaws in both hands and forced my mouth open. "We'll have to do something about those teeth. And your throat's not deep enough. Well, you'll just have to do. I need a quick replacement for tonight's shift. One of my best pussy mouths got choked to death this afternoon on a stallion dick, and I have lots of business coming in tonight."

He reached into his pocket and pulled out two soft rubber tooth protectors like the kind boxers wear. He fitted them over both my upper and lower teeth. Then he produced a very long and thick cucumber. "Open wide!" he commanded as he began to force it into my mouth. I yanked my wrists against the handcuffs helplessly as the cucumber invaded my defenseless throat.

"You've got to take it all and close your lips," he said, forcing it in slowly but firmly. To my surprise, it seemed to gradually glide down my throat, like a sword swallower's act at the carnival. I closed my lips around the massive invader. I could feel it bulging against the soft tissues of my mouth and esophagus.

"Good boy!" said the Sukmaster. "Just leave it there for a few minutes to stretch that pussy mouth while I check your schedule for tonight." He pulled a small white book from his shirt pocket and began to read.

"Midnight until three in the morning is your shift, cuntface," he began. "You get the last toilet stall, the one with three glory holes. Now, let's see. There's Farmer John and his son, Butch. They're regulars at Susie's Suck Stop. They always come in together, one night a week. They save up a week's worth of spunk and blast it out all at once, and tonight's the night. Aren't you lucky? They've been thinking about it for the whole week, looking forward to the night when they blast it down some nerd's throat. You can service them in any order you want. They're both mule-dicked dudes in shit-stained overalls, one young, and one older, naturally, since they're father and son. They're both towheaded blonds, and the hair on their big testicles is curly and silvery gold. Treat them re-e-eal nice!"

I looked up at the neon sign flashing above the parking lot. It indeed read SUSIE'S SUCK STOP. I had been mistaken before. Now I was again.

The Sukmaster continued. "Also, there's Devil Dong Dan. He's a redheaded dude and a dirty-dicked biker. You'll smell him before you see him. He's all over in dirty black leather and straps and chains. He'll keep his helmet on with the faceplate shut while he fucks your face; he likes the feeling of oxygen deprivation when he flushes his turgid testicles.

"And last, but definitely not least, there's Brutus Bodoni, an olive-skinned, curly black-haired Greek-Sicilian-American truck driver who stays wired on stimulants for cross-country marathon no-sleep drives and ends up his haul at SUSIE'S SUCK STOP for a much-needed private tongue bath. His baseball-bat dick stays rock-hard from the moment he shoves it through the glory hole till the time he shoots you about a good four ounces of road-flavored sperm. Hope you're hungry!

"Plus, you can suck off any unscheduled studs who happen to walk in. Extras!"

The Sukmaster snapped the appointment book shut and put it into his shirt pocket. "Speaking of which, how are you doing with that cucumber down your throat? Are you having fun yet?"

"Mepilvit. Gmphmr." I moved my head only slightly because the cucumber was like a thick ramrod down my throat.

"Excellent!" said the Sukmaster. He fastened a dog collar around my swollen throat and led me on a leash through the back parking lot. Jenkins had vanished into the darkness. I shuffled on all fours across the old curled-up shit-colored plastic tile of the men's pissoir. I saw some pairs of legs inside the first toilet stalls. The Sukmaster led me to the final stall and forcefully seated me on the bare toilet, which had no seat. My handcuffed hands were fastened to the toilet pipes behind me with a sturdy steel swivel clamp. I had just enough freedom of movement to work all three glory holes. I was glad that my khaki trousers were not pulled down, because they protected my butt from the icy-cold seatless toilet.

My hard dick was straining against the crotch of my pants, unable to escape the cloth. The Sukmaster closed and latched the door of the stall from the outside. I leaned back against the toilet pipes and looked down at my body, my T-shirt pulled tight against my chest, my khaki pants pulled taut at the crotch by the vague outline of my imprisoned erection. I needed to rub my dick against something—anything. There was only the cloth of my khakis. I was horny as a goat from thinking about the Sukmaster's appointment book.

I began to writhe up and down from the hips, twisting in an attempt to rub the head of my dick against the cloth. I needed stimulation really bad. When would my first customer arrive? I needed my throat empty! I leaned forward and started to heave and choke, trying to force the cucumber out. It came out with devastating slowness. All the tissues of my mouth and throat and tongue were slightly swollen and engorged with blood as a result of the elixirs in the cucumber. As the last of the cucumber emerged from my lips, my first customers arrived.

I stretched forward and put my eye to the three-inch glory hole in the door of the stall. Two big guys were standing at the urinal, pissing, with their backs to me. These must be some of the extras the Sukmaster said I could take if I wanted and if I could get them to give me their loads. I put my lips to the hole. I didn't want the guys in the other stalls to get these dudes first. "Psst!" I said. My dick was bursting in my pants. "You guys need your dicks sucked?" I put my eye back to the hole. My throat was throbbing from the cucumber. I needed it filled up real fast. One of the guys turned around from the urinal so that I could see his dick, which wasn't hard at all but already prime suckable meat for the starving cock slave.

No need for words. I wanted that man's dick. I put my pussy mouth against the hole and ran my swollen tongue in and out through my cuntlike lips. His jackboots thumped the cheap flooring as he advanced to shove his prick in my mouth. His limp flesh hardened in seconds under the forceful movements of my soft, swollen tongue. His expanding cock slid quickly to the back of my mouth while I chewed against the hairy base with my rubber-clad teeth. A dozen well-placed thrusts of his loins, and this horny dude fed my parched throat with a satisfying shower of sperm before he withdrew, saying to his buddy at the urinal, "Pretty damn good suck job. You oughta try it out, Jack."

"Aww, no. I don't think so."

"Jack, listen to me. This fruit's got a great technique." Then he lowered his voice to a whisper I could just barely hear. "It don't make you a queer to get your dick sucked. Only the guy who sucks it is a queer. Look at me. Am I a queer?"

"No."

"Then go over there and get your dick sucked."

He pushed his buddy by the shoulders over to the glory hole. Jack's fine, fat, tan, thick dick came closer and closer, dangling through the fly of his blue jeans. I darted my tongue through the glory hole until it met the head of his cock. Then I began to calf-lick his cock in big slurps. He didn't take much convincing, because his dick roared up like a lion and shot a major wad after about only five seconds of licking. It never even made it through the glory hole. He buttoned up, and he and his friend exited, laughing.

I was really disappointed that I missed most of his jizz bomb, so I licked what I could get off the door of the stall around the hole by stretching my tongue from the inside and licking around the rim. I was doing this when my next customer arrived.

The musty smell of sweat, dirty leather, axle grease, and beer and the clinking sound of chains on his boots and shoulders accompanied his stroll toward the first stall, farthest from where I was chained to the plumbing. Devil Dong Dan bent over and looked through the first stall's glory hole.

"Howya doin'?" Devil Dog Dan said. "Where's my date?"

"He's in the last stall tonight, Dan," a voice said. "A new one. He's real hungry. Sucked two dicks already, and the shift's just started. This one's chained by his wrists behind him to the plumbing because he's an animal. That's all he is—a cocksucking animal."

"My dick's starting to get crazy just thinking about the very word *suck*." He stomped over to the last stall, where I had my eye glued to the hole. Devil Dong Dan unsnapped the leather codpiece of his biker pants. His swollen prick flopped out. Like most redheaded studs, his meat was thick and white with a purple head trying to slide out of its foreskin sheath. He eased it through the glory hole in the door. I stared at its magnificent girth and watched as it slowly came to attention. Its thickness filled the entire diameter of the hole. I leaned forward, straining against my chained wrists.

As the swollen, plumlike head emerged, I could see and smell a coating of road smegma around the edges, yellow-beige and cheesy. "My prick needs a good cleaning, pussyface, so start lickin'," Dan growled. His voice was muffled inside the closed visor of his helmet.

I extended my swollen tongue and started licking. The smegma tasted of Camembert and asphalt. After I had licked the entire head clean, I ran the tip of my tongue around the crevices of the retracted foreskin.

"Turn around so I can shove this thing up your butt," Dan's muffled voice commanded.

"I can't turn around. My wrists are handcuffed to the pipes."

"OK, then get that fucker down your throat," he ordered. I strained forward and started to ease Dan's dong down my throat. The previous two dicks were just an appetizer. This was really a meal. The throbbing mass quickly filled my mouth as the mammoth head forced its way deep into my tender esophagus. Miraculously, I could still breathe somehow.

With a quick movement of his hips, Dan completely withdrew his prick from my mouth-cunt and then stabbed it in again its full length. I strained forward to receive the full inward thrust. The entire length plunged deeper into my straining throat. The engorged tissues welcomed this powerful thrusting massage.

Dan withdrew once more and again plunged his thick cock to the hilt down my eager throat. Again and again he withdrew and plunged forward. His breathing came fast and heavy as the nitrogen level inside his helmet increased. This was real face-fucking, with no holds barred whatsoever. The flesh of my mouth and throat swelled against the invading dick, becoming burning hot, like a chili attack.

"Unh! U-u-unh! *U-u-unnh!*" Devil Dong Dan moaned as he thrust his hips a few final times. A burning hot blast of sperm hit my esophagus. Dan's dick was still spurting jism as he withdrew, spraying my face and the front of my T-shirt. Then he plunged his prick in again to deliver a few more jolts of hot come directly into my throat. Finally he drew back from the glory hole, leaving a trail of cream running down the door.

I leaned forward to lick this extra come off the rough stained plywood door. I noticed two words written on the wood with a ballpoint pen. They read, WHAT'S REAL?

I heard Dan's greasy boots clomp a few steps back as he fastened the chrome snaps on his leather codpiece. "Good head!" he said as he made for the door. I leaned back to relieve the pressure on my handcuffed arms. My T-shirt front and pants were covered with sticky gobs of spilled semen, and my own cock was straining against the tight cloth of my khakis. I needed to stroke my cock, but my hands could not be freed. With a sigh I leaned forward and looked through the glory hole.

Two men were standing at the urinals, both wearing manure-stained coveralls, both tall, husky towheaded blonds. I knew they were Farmer John and his son, Butch. They were talking in low voices that I could just make out.

"That's one hell of a hard-on, Butch," said Farmer John. "You ain't been pullin' on it at all this week, huh?"

"No, Pa. I been savin' it for our regular blow session tonight. My nuts are achin' with a really big load of come. Look."

Butch turned around to face his dad. He pulled down the crotch of his coveralls and let fall out an immense set of swollen testicles covered with soft gold hairs. His farm-boy mule dick was already hard and ready for action. "I ain't never seen my nuts so full of come!" he said.

Farmer John turned to face his son. His own dick was twitching and throbbing. He was slowly massaging it with one hand while with the other he reached down and cradled his son's nuts in one callused palm.

"They sure feel heavy to me," he said. "Maybe you gonna blast the back of that cocksucker's head off when you come." They both chuckled. Farmer John continued to massage his son's nuts.

"Take a feel of mine, Butch." Butch reached down and pulled his dad's testicles from his baggy coveralls. If anything, they were as swollen as his son's.

"Gee, Pop, you sure got a load too." He looked down with admiration as he slowly massaged his dad's engorged gonads. The farmer's enormous dick stood straight up, slowly leaking precome.

"You wanna go first?" Farmer John asked. "I like to hear you groan when you shoot your load. Makes me real horny. Like to hear that cocksucker gag when he tries to swaller all that come."

"Nah, Pop, you go first. I went first last week." Butch gave a playful tug on his dad's testicles.

"Tell ya what, Butch," Farmer John replied. "There's a hole in the door, and there's a hole in the next stall. Let's shove our peters in at the same time and let that pussy-faced cocksucker decide which one he wants to suck first."

"OK, Pa, sounds like fun!" Butch turned and walked over to the stall next to mine as Farmer John approached the door through which I was peeking.

Simultaneously two mighty, hard pricks thrust themselves into my stall. Farmer John's came through the glory hole in front of me, and Butch's came through the hole to my right. I licked my lips in anticipation of this double feast of turgid turkey neck.

But which one to suck first?

I decided to suck both at once. Why not?

I gave the dad's cock a couple of preliminary licks and heard his grunt of satisfaction. Then I turned to Butch's twitching rod and gave it a couple of preliminary licks as well. I heard him draw in his breath. "Phew! That's real good. He's suckin' my dick first, Pop!" he chortled.

"No he ain't, he's suckin' my dick right now!" Farmer John said, and I was. By the time Farmer John replied, I had plunged his big thick dick right to the back of my hot throat. These thick farm tools were so long that their heads almost met in the middle of the stall in front of my mouth. So I hadn't far to move as I filled my swollen throat first with the father and then with the son in a steady rhythm of come hunger. Slimy threads of precome started to slide down their dicks as I worked my cocksucker's lips and tongue along the shafts.

"He likes my dick better'n yours, Pop," heaved Butch in preorgasmic sighs.

"You're lyin', you big hornbill!" grunted Farmer John, his big mule dick throbbing under the assault of my cunt-mouth. "He likes my dick better, 'cause he's suckin' the shit out of it!"

I could tell that these big studs were about to let fly with their loads, so I redoubled my efforts in an increased rhythm, plunging my head down on the daddy's dick and then to my right on the son's. I heard them both begin to groan, and then the come began to fly.

I pulled back and positioned my open mouth in the crossfire. Blast after blast of hot white cream spattered my eyes, nose, cheeks, and chin, then streamed down the front of my already-sticky T-shirt. Moans of satisfaction from behind the shaking partitions accompanied these sperm torrents.

My eager mouth was filled several times over with fresh hot farmer's cream. I swallowed and waited for more, and there was more than enough to fill my waiting gorge several times over. As a parting shot, I licked their softening pricks as clean as I could.

"Hey, Pop, did you come yet?" asked Butch breathlessly.

"Sure did, son," he replied. "Damn fine suck job."

The now-flaccid pricks withdrew from the glory holes. "I can't wait till next week," said Farmer John as he and Butch buttoned up their coveralls.

"Me neither, Pop," came the reply.

I sat back and looked at myself. I really was a mess of half-dried and fresh, slimy jism. Big wads of it hung off my cheeks and chin; I tried unsuccessfully to lick them off with my tongue. My T-shirt was stuck to my chest, and the front of my khakis was completely soaked. My rock-hard dick still strained for release. I needed to shoot my own wad real bad, but there was no way. My bound hands were completely helpless behind me.

I heard the latrine door slam as Farmer John and Butch left. I waited, my mouth and throat burning from the physical abuse they had been given. The sweet-salty taste of five huge sperm loads lingered on, making me realize that my cunt-mouth needed even more. I didn't have long to wait.

I heard a great roar from the parking lot. I looked through the glory hole in the wall to my left. It gave direct access to the outside wall of the building. It was for curb service, for those trucker studs in a hurry who didn't want to even take the time to walk inside, whose big sperm sacs had been superstimulated by hours and days of nonstop driving and pills, and who needed mouth service real fast with no nonsense.

I could see a huge red diesel squealing to a halt just a few yards from my suck hole. The chrome glinted through a faint cloud of dust from the dirty tires. The brakes hissed. Painted letters in gold and black on the driver's door read BRUTUS BODONI—NONSTOP DELIVERIES.

The door opened, and Brutus swung down to the asphalt. This monster stud's huge frame bulged out of tattered jeans and stretched a black tank top to its limit, beginning to split the seams. His huge thighs bulged through the thin, worn denim of his Levi's. His forearms resembled Smithfield hams, but covered with curly black hair. The tendons of his thick bull neck glistened with sweat. He scratched at his four-day growth of tough black beard, stretched, and yawned.

My eyes were riveted to Brutus's crotch. Whatever the fascinations the rest of his massive physique held, his crotch was the feature presentation. Through the thin, faded denim, a sausage shape bulged out to the left and down his thigh halfway to his knee. On the other side of the button fly, the two globes of his gonads strained through the cloth like two small melons.

He strode over to the curb-service glory hole, and without a word started to undo the straining buttons of his Levi's. Then he unbuckled the thick leather belt and peeled the tight jeans down to his hairy thighs. The great testicles fell out and swung down halfway to his knees, and his massive cock shot upward, as big as my forearm. He shoved the head of his big organ against the glory hole.

Unfortunately, it was too thick to go through the hole.

Brutus pulled back, and then with a mighty shove of his pelvis, he rammed his rigid pile driver against the hole again. I heard the splintering of wood on the outside wall. Then he rammed again, and the Sheetrock of the inside wall cracked and fell away in powdery chunks to the floor. Brutus's huge cock finally plowed through, leaving a ragged hole in both the outside and inside walls. It towered above my face, hard as a rock, its blue veins throbbing menacingly.

I started to give the thick shaft a tongue bath, licking it clean of gypsum dust and wood flakes. I couldn't reach the dick head from my seated position on the toilet, so I had to raise myself up a few inches off the seat with my knees flexed. I tried to get my mouth around the tip, but there was no way. It was too big.

"Suck my dick!" Brutus yelled.

I knew what I had to do. I unhinged my lower jaw like a snake who swallows a victim many times its own girth. Then I gradually eased my head onto the massive, pulsating prick shaft. My already tortured throat burned and throbbed with the agony of ingesting this huge intruder. Brutus began to groan. "That's it, get down on that fucker!" His hips began to heave as he attempted to force his cock farther down my throat. I eased it down until my face was pressing against the ragged hole in the wall.

Without warning, the already-cracked panel gave way, and my head broke through the Sheetrock. Now I was truly all the way down on the entire unbelievable length of Brutus's prick. My lips pressed against the wooden boards of the outer wall. My knees were weak with the effort of holding my body in this tortured position, my arms stretched behind me and chained to the plumbing. I gave way with my knees but did not move, because my jaws were locked around the thick mass of Brutus's cock.

I was literally impaled on his prick.

My face was trapped in the ragged hole in the wall like a vise.

Then he began to prick-pound my trapped face. Over and over his brutal thrusts rammed the rock-hard prick deep down into my helpless, tender throat. I wanted to scream in agony, but no sound would emerge. The strain was so enormous that my own cock burst out of the fly of my khaki pants.

"Get ready for a big load, faggot!" he yelled. One last superthrust, and I felt scalding-hot lava pour down my throat and into my guts. My own dick began to spurt wads of creamy jism in a simultaneous orgasm as I felt Brutus spend the last of his lust into my innards.

He pulled out with such sudden force that I fell down onto the toilet like a rag doll, dazed and weak. His streaming cock had left a thick trail of come down my chin and the broken wall. I was too weak to lick it up. I leaned back against the cold plumbing and stared at the dirty ceiling of the latrine. I heard the door of Brutus's truck cab slam, the hiss of air as the brakes released, and a roar as he took off into the night.

I looked at the graffito on the door. WHAT'S REAL? it read.

After that, I realized what was going on. I was and had been in a vivid dream, and now I was lucid. I easily willed my hands free from the handcuffs and walked out of the latrine into the misty night. A full moon beamed overhead.

I looked down at myself. I was wearing an old-style sailor's uniform: white with a thirteen-button drop front. A little way down the highway, I saw a man standing under a streetlight. He was walking a small dragon on a leash.

I walked up to him and asked, "Where is this?"

"Kama Loka, naturally!" was his reply. He pointed up over our heads. How had I not noticed the metal archway with blue neon letters glowing against the black sky? It read, WELCOME TO KAMA LOKA—DREAM CITY OF DESIRE.

The man with the dragon smiled and looked down at my crotch.

PART TWO

So this was what it was like to be in a lucid dream. Everything seemed very real and yet strange, shifting and ambiguous. The arch of neon letters overhead shed its weird blue light on the highway: WELCOME TO KAMA LOKA—DREAM CITY OF DESIRE. The man with the dragon on the leash smiled as he stared at my crotch. "You must be a stranger here," he said. The little dragon yawned, its mouth disgorging a puff of flame that evaporated in the damp night air.

I needed to contact Dr. Wünder. I moved my fingers as if typing: *Am I dreaming?*

I immediately felt a short tingle at the corners of my eyes. One short meant "yes." Dr. Wünder had replied through the Lucid Dream Monitor. *Am now in Kama Loka,* I typed.

I was definitely in a lucid dream. I decided to attempt to control the flow of events. I knew that the man I was talking to was a revegen—a dream creature. I had to find out more about him and about Kama Loka.

I looked up at the moon beaming eerily through the mist. "Full moon tonight," I ventured.

"It's always a full moon in Kama Loka, stranger." He paused. "Except when it's not."

This seemed to make perfect sense. "Where *is* Kama Loka?" I asked. I didn't want to seem too nosy at first.

"Why, right here!" he said, waving his arm in a wide gesture. "Kama Loka is right here—where we are."

This was not what I wanted to know. I tried again.

"Is Kama Loka...real?" I asked.

"What's real?" replied the man with the dragon. He smiled.

This kind of question-and-answer method was getting me nowhere. I decided to take another approach. Maybe I could find someone in charge who could give me more information.

"Can I see the ruler of Kama Loka?" I asked.

"Sure—it's right here," he answered. He reached into his pocket and produced a folding carpenter's ruler. "Let's see what your status is." I looked down as he grasped my dick, discovering that my trousers had disappeared and that I had a full, throbbing erection. He deftly took a measurement. "Hmm...a little small, stranger. But you're in luck. We're right near the Sexarcade, one of the most desirable parts of town. Come along with me—I'll take you to the Penis Enhancement Parlor!"

He took my arm, and we drifted through the misty night of Kama Loka. Shadowy shapes in the distance resolved themselves into human forms as we approached. The denizens of the City of Desire were out for an evening stroll under illuminated signs that flashed their bright colors through the gray night mist.

On my left I saw the Aphrodisia Café. SNACKS & APHRODISIACS read the sign above the door. I stopped to look at the menu in the window:

EELS IN JALAPEÑO JUICE—
    FOR RED-HOT HARD-ONS . . . . .12 UD
CHAMPAGNE SWEETBREADS—
    LOAD UP YOUR GONADS . . . . .17 UD
HUMMINGBIRD TESTICLE TORTE—
    CREAMY YET FLAKY . . . . .15 UD
PEACOCK EGG OMELETTE—
    CHOCK FULL OF HORMONES . . . . .10 UD
TARTARE OF MOUNTAIN OYSTERS—
    'NUFF SAID . . . . .22 UD
SPECIAL OF THE EVENING—
    BUFFALO PENIS FRICASSEE . . . . .6 UD

I turned to my guide. "What's 'UD'?" I asked.

"Units of desire," he explained. "It's what things cost in Kama Loka. You want some, stranger?" He handed me a small purple velvet drawstring purse. Inside I found dozens of dime-size gold coins, each with a square hole in the center.

"Do I have to earn these?" I was a bit suspicious.

"No, they're free for the time being. You pay up when you leave Kama Loka."

What did I have to lose? I was directing this dream, wasn't I? I tucked the purse in my pocket. My trousers were back.

"I'm hungry," I announced. "I think I'll get the special of the evening."

"Well, they don't allow dragons in the Aphrodisia Café, so I'll say good night for now. The Penis Enhancement Parlor is right up the street in the Sexarcade." He pointed ahead to a vague glow of colored lights in the mist. He waved good-bye as he disappeared into the night.

A waiter emerged as I sat down at an empty table. "Hi! I'm Bruce, and I'll be your waiter this evening." He stared ahead and tapped his foot. "Well, I'm waiting!"

"I'll have the special of the evening," I said.

"Ah, the buffalo penis fricassee in testosterone sauce. An excellent choice, monsieur." He whisked forward a big steaming platter from behind his back and placed it on the table. A knife and fork appeared. Bruce tied a big white bib around my neck.

"Boner appetit!" he called out, flitting away.

The oversize platter framed a huge tubular hunk of purplish pink penis, perhaps three inches in diameter and about sixteen inches long, smothered in a thick, creamy beige sauce. I removed the parsley and threw it over my shoulder. I sliced off a big hunk and started to chew.

Mmm! A string quartet began to play on the mezzanine. Delicious! I sliced again and stuffed another chunk into my mouth. I was famished. Why had I never tasted buffalo penis before? Delicious juices trickled down my throat as I chewed. It was a bit salty and somewhat like the tenderest pork tenderloin with a slightly gamy overtone.

"Garçon!" I shouted. "Vino!"

Bruce appeared with a bottle and wineglass and began pouring a deep red vintage. "Château Cockadoodledoo, 1937," he said. "Oh, boy, wait until you get the check!"

I took a deep gulp. Superb! My appetite was equal to the huge dish before me. Soon enough the platter was empty. I belched and rose from the table. The aphrodisiac effect of the dinner was apparent. My erect cock and swollen balls strained through my trousers.

"Your check, monsieur," Bruce said. "Seventy-seven units of desire, *s'il vous plaît.*"

"Isn't that a little expensive?" I asked.

"Whatever you say, monsieur," Bruce replied, tearing the check into little bits of confetti and tossing them over his head. He fell to his knees and kissed my feet; then he kissed my crotch. "Au revoir, monsieur!" he called as I drifted up the way to the Sex-arcade. I could see that you had to be firm with these revegens.

Up ahead a riot of garishly colored signs touted their messages the length of the arcade while shadowy revegens strolled about. I noticed that their features seemed to resolve only when I looked directly at them. The doorman on my right emerged from the mist and took my arm. "Like something a little wild?" he asked, pointing to the sign overhead. It read MOTHER GOOSE'S SUITE. I studied the colored pictures in the displays.

SHEPHERD'S DELITE, read one. A ewe with long eyelashes and a smear of crimson lipstick on her muzzle presented her rump and looked coyly over her shoulder. The picture animated as she batted her eyelashes and sheepishly crooned, "Come out and see me sometime…come out and see me sometime…"

A picture of a giraffe with a throbbing erection proclaimed: GET AEROBIC WITH JERRY GIRAFFE! BETWEEN THE KISSING AND THE SUCKING, YOU'LL RUN FIVE MILES!

SO HORNY YOU COULD HONK? TRY GUY THE GOOSE! read another display. I also noticed ENGLEBERT ELEPHANT—FOR REAL CHUBBY-CHASERS. Butch Baboon boasted a bright blue boner. And next to him was, HE'S A THRILLA! CHAUNCEY GORILLA!

Then the display for Teddy the Bear caught my attention. Teddy's picture showed a disturbing furry mix of stuffed-toy cuteness and primeval grizzly power. Below the picture was an equally disturbing little poem:

My love's a cuddly Teddy Bear
Completely clad in soft brown hair.
His hairy paws are pink inside;
His chest is broad, his shoulders wide.

I lay my head upon his belly,
Which quivers like a hairy jelly,
And stroke his thick and furry bone
Until it spurts. I hear him moan.

Then lighted by the silvery moon,
I feed him honey from a spoon,
And nestling 'gainst his fuzzy chest,
I fall asleep; and so we rest,

Until at golden blush of dawn,
When I awake to find him gone.

The doorman was looking down at the outline of my semierect dick, which was making an obscene show as it pressed against the crotch of my white pants.

"*Psst!*" hissed the doorman in my ear. "Looks like you need to get together with Teddy the Bear. Only 75 UDs."

It sounded like fun, but I was getting distracted. "Maybe some other time," I replied as I drifted away up the Sexarcade. "There's something I have to do." I simply had to locate the Penis Enhancement Parlor, of which as yet I had seen no trace.

I was beginning to worry that I wasn't really controlling this lucid dream. The garish displays of the Sexarcade were distracting me no end. I looked up to see the sign KINGDOM OF KINK! spelled out in acid green and orange. Chains and whips dangled on hooks from the eaves. Farther on I spied CYBERSIBLINGS—DOUBLE YOUR PLEASURE! This captioned a picture showing twin studs of Adonis-like male beauty, fitted with thick chrome bands at their necks, biceps, wrists, waists, thighs, and ankles. The signs flashed on all sides:

BOY-GIRL BOUTIQUE—CAN'T MAKE UP YOUR MIND?
GET BOTH IN ONE BODY IN OUR HERMAPHRODITE HAREM.

TEMPLE OF PRIAPUS—
SERVICES EVERY HOUR ON THE HOUR—
ORGIASTIC RITUAL AT MIDNIGHT.
CUM AND BE SAVED, BROTHER!

Suddenly, there it was! Big, blocky red letters on the marquee read P.E.P., and beneath, in smaller type: PENIS ENHANCEMENT PARLOR. I examined the sign next to the door.

YOUR BEST BARGAIN
DR. HUNG SOO FAT, M.S.G.
(MASTER OF SEXUAL GEOMETRY)
DIRECT FROM HONG KONG
NO JOB TOO BIG OR TOO SMALL

The door was of quilted pink satin with a small porthole window at eye level. I looked through the window to confront the face of a Chinese sage peering back at me. Dr. Hung Soo Fat, without a doubt. His voice came muffled through the door: "You no be disappointed!" I pulled open the door.

"So you're from Hong Kong, Doctor?" I asked him.

"Ahhh, no," he replied. "That misplint on sign. I flom *Dong* Kong." He smiled ambiguously. "Light this way, Mr. Stlange." He took my arm and led me to the pink-satin-covered operating table at the back of the room. "You please to undless and lecline." In a trice I found myself naked and flat on my back. Dr. Hung Soo Fat slipped on a pair of shocking-pink rubber gloves and began to examine my prick under the strong overhead lights.

He tugged at a tuft of my pubic hair. "Why you not dye you hai'ah? You look much bettah as ledhead. Hai'ah tint only five unit of desi'ah. Special tonight." He looked at me expectantly.

I had to start taking control of this dream. I wasn't here to change the color of my pubic hair. "What else can you do, Dr.

Hung?" I queried. He pointed one shocking-pink finger to a large handwritten sign on the wall. "There plice list. You pick, I do the tlick," he giggled. I read the list.

DICK STRETCH (PER INCH)	.50 UD
DICK THICKEN	
(PER QUARTER-INCH DIAMETER)	.25 UD
HEAD GLOSS	.15 UD
HEAD COLORS:	
PURPLE	.10 UD
MAROON	.12 UD
APRICOT	.25 UD
CHERRY-RED	.30 UD
SHAFT TINTING (SPECIFY COLOR: ALABASTER,	
MAUVE, PECAN, OR EBONY)	.35 UD
CUSTOM COLORS, ADD	.10 UD
ARTISTIC VEINING (PER VEIN; SPECIFY TINT:	
BLUISH, PURPLISH, OR REDDISH)	.12 UD
CUSTOM PUBIC HAIR COLOR	.20 UD
SUPER COMBINATION	.150 UD

"What's the Super Combo, Dr. Hung?" I asked.

"That evelything above...and mo'ah," he answered. He began to expertly massage my turgid prick with his lithe hands.

"I'll take the Super Combo," I gasped in anticipation. "Give me the longest, fattest, most beautiful dick in Kama Loka."

"Ahhh! You go for bloke! Good! Now you need pick hues and tints," he said as he began to forcefully pull my dick upward. It felt wonderful. I lay back against the pink satin pillow and imagined my enhanced penis. "Let's see, I'll take the alabaster shaft with thick bluish veins, the cherry-red head with a very glossy finish, and color my pubic hair jet-black and make it short, thick, and very curly."

There was a little sniff of disapproval from Dr. Hung. "Why you no color you hai'ah led? Look extlemely nice. Make pubic hai'ah match chelly-led head. OK?"

115

"No, I want jet-black!" I insisted. Whose dream was this, anyway? I needed to assert myself more firmly. These revegens were trying to have their own way. "Black!" I repeated.

"OK, OK!" Dr. Hung relented. "Jet-black it is. No get upset!" He began to slather my erect dick with an icy-cold syrup. As he pulled and heaved, the shaft began to lengthen like soft taffy, and yet it seemed not to lose its thickness. "You get fifteen-inch plick...two inches long'ah than longest lecolded plick in Kama Loka." He finished by releasing my dick. It was so long that it couldn't stand up straight, and it flopped down on my chest. Dr. Hung now inserted a tube into my dick hole. "Now I make thick," he explained. "Need make thick to stand up nice and stiff."

A viscous, clear, icy liquid flowed into my dick from the tube, and I watched in amazement as the organ slowly started to swell and thicken. It tingled all over, outside and within, as the tissues expanded. Soon it was as big around as a beer can. "You say when," said Dr. Hung. I let it swell for a few minutes more before I said, "OK. Stop." It was pretty damn thick—and standing straight up.

"Now I do tinting," Dr. Hung said as he produced a small airbrush and began spray-painting my prick. A miraculous transformation took place before my eyes as the ordinary, mousy coloration of my previously nerdy dick began to gleam with vivid color. The cherry-red and very glossy head seemed to pulsate in contrast to the pure, warm, translucent white of the alabaster dick shaft. My choice was vindicated—the jet-black pubic hair surrounding the pale shaft was a dynamite combination. Red, white, and black. A knockout in more ways than one.

Dr. Hung Soo Fat stopped spraying and stepped back to admire his work. "You bettah off with black," he said apologetically. I sat up and swung my legs off the table. I couldn't wait to show this beauty around town. The doctor grabbed my shoulders and pushed me back down. "You not leady yet! Need to do family jewels! Make big and heavy. I fill up with sex-dlive sylup. What flavah you like?"

"Sex-drive syrup? Flavor? What flavors do you have?"

116

Dr. Hung furrowed his brow. "Have stlawbelly, chelly, laspbelly, olange, nectaline, glape—"

"Those are all so fruity," I interrupted. "Do you have vanilla?"

He shook his head sorrowfully. "Ahhh! Too bad, no vanilla...maybe you like Locky Load?"

I was losing control again. I had to be more decisive. "OK, give me Rocky Road." I relaxed my head on the pink satin. I felt a little jab in both my nuts as Dr. Hung stuck tubes deep into the tissues. I saw the thick, chocolaty liquid flow into my gonads. I felt the immeasurable pleasure of their swelling as the sex drive pumped them up, filling every fiber and capillary.

"I give you enough fo'ah five big loads," said Dr. Hung. "Plenty fo'ah one evening on town."

I lifted myself up on my elbows and looked with amazement at my inflated testicles. Magnificent! Huge!

"Maybe you'd better stop, Dr. Hung. I might have trouble walking."

"Ahhh! Maybe too big. You want I take some out?" he asked.

"No, no, that's OK. Just don't put any more in." I sensed he was trying to take control again.

He yanked the tubes out of my balls. "All finish! You lookin' good!" He gave my new megameat a few friendly slaps. I sat up and swung my legs off the table.

My admiration for Dr. Hung Soo Fat's artistry knew no bounds. With the engorgement of my testicles, the effect was complete. The coloration of my huge prick glowed against the dusky mass of my mammoth balls; the genital trio hung over the edge of the operating table almost to my knees. I stood up on my feet for the first time since the procedure began.

And immediately staggered forward. I fell right into the arms of Dr. Hung, who kept me from falling flat on my face. "You bettah watch out," he warned. "You gotta lotta extla weight in flont for a skinny guy." He held my shoulders while I took a few tentative steps. I definitely felt front-heavy—it was an alien sensation, to be sure. I straightened my back and spread my legs a bit for balance. I simply needed a little practice with my magnificent new equipment. Now I was eager to explore Kama Loka—Dream City of Desire.

"Well, thanks, Dr. Hung," I said. "I guess I'll be going."

He looked surprised as he replied, "Wait! You not leady yet. Need outfit." He dug into an old footlocker and handed me an elastic jockstrap with an oversize pouch. It fit well enough, except that portions of my nuts tried to escape from the sides. At least it kept them and my massive, dangling dong from interfering with my walking. Yes, it was definitely easier to walk with the jock's support.

Next, Dr. Hung handed me a voluminous black cloak. I pulled it over my shoulders and clasped it at the neck. I pulled it shut to cover the big, bulging pouch of the jockstrap. Even when the cloak was closed, there could be seen a swelling in front that indicated that something unusual was going on beneath.

"You tly not get election when jockstlap is on. It might lip." He smiled mischievously. "Now you pay bill: one hundled fifty UD, please."

I took my purse from the pile of discarded clothes and began to count out the small gold coins. "That sounds terribly expensive, Dr. Hung," I told him.

He looked at me with a frown, then he brightened. "OK," he said, "we levalue Kama Loka money. Each coin now stand fo'ah ten UD. You pay only fifteen coin." He held out his hand in an emphatic gesture, and I laid fifteen small gold coins in his palm. My throbbing prick and balls could barely be contained by the elastic pouch of the jockstrap, and I was anxious to be on my way to unknown adventures.

But I was supposed to be doing research about Kama Loka! I needed more information. "Dr. Hung, is there someone in charge here?" I asked.

He frowned and cogitated, his nostrils quivering. "You mean, like, who tell you what to do?"

"Yes, that's it exactly! Who is it?"

"You maybe need tly Domination Den, acloss stleet. They extlemely bossy over the'ah."

"No, no, no. Not sexual domination, Dr. Hung." I thought for a moment. "Is there a mayor in Kama Loka?"

He thought for a moment. "May'ah…may'ah… Ahhh! We gotta lotta nightmay'ah. Maybe you want see one?"

"No, no, no. Just forget it, Dr. Hung. Thanks for the beautiful job. You've outdone yourself." I made for the satin-quilted front door and pushed my way out into the misty night. The purse was tucked into a little pocket in my cloak. I had money, a huge dick, full nuts, and I was out on the town!

"You have lip-loaring time, Stlange'ah!" exhorted Dr. Hung as I staggered away.

I was heading for the bright lights farther down the Sexarcade. I noticed a young man standing in the shadows, leaning against a storefront. I walked up to him and asked, "You want to see a really big dick?" I was perhaps too eager.

"Not particularly," he yawned.

"I mean a really, really, *really* big dick," I persisted. I was learning that one had to be assertive with these revegens.

"Well, OK," he said. I pulled open the cloak and yanked aside the elastic pouch of the jockstrap, letting my amazing, colossal cock and behemoth balls fall out. The young man gazed down for a moment, then opened his throat in piercing shrieks and disappeared into the misty night.

This was fun! I left the black folds of the cloak parted slightly and continued up the street. I focused on a figure lying in the gutter. His golden hair and pale body glistened with droplets of condensed mist. On his back was written with bright red lipstick: WILL WORK FOR SEX.

I prodded him with my toe to get his attention. "Hey," I said, "I've got something for you."

He sat up and squinted at me with the most innocent-looking blue eyes I'd ever seen. Then his gaze fastened on the crotch spectacle taking place behind the partially open cloak. His eyes brightened as he stared.

"Oh, man!" he murmured. "Oh, man, oh, man, oh, *man!* Can I see more of that thing?"

119

I pulled the front of the cloak open completely. Blond Angel reached gingerly forward with both his pale hands. "What an incredible dick on such a skinny little guy! Man, oh, man! Can I touch it?"

"Sure," I said. "Be my guest."

He began to stroke the alabaster shaft with both hands, from top to bottom, like stroking a cat. Then he began to nibble gently at the knotty bluish veins with his lips and tongue. He looked up at me from his knees. "Wow!" he intoned. "This is really heavy-duty meat, stranger!"

By this time Megameat was halfway erect and pointing directly at Blond Angel's mouth. He opened his lips and sucked up a few drops of precome from the cherry-red head. Then he put both hands around the massive shaft—one hand wouldn't have even begun to reach around it—and began to work up and down, milking my meat, hoping for more sex juices to appear from the dick hole so he might suck up more of his favorite nectar.

Megameat was now fully erect, and Blond Angel had to stand up to continue his ministrations. He tugged at, pushed against, and milked the shaft and was soon rewarded with a small dribble of dark brown liquid.

"Oh, boy!" he said. "I love Rocky Road!" He bent over and licked up every last drop from the shiny dick head like a kid licking a bowl of frosting. My dick meat was throbbing preorgasmically, and my big nuts were contracting and pulsating. "I need more of that good sex juice," Blond Angel panted, redoubling his stimulating efforts.

He wrapped both hands around the shaft again, still barely able to encircle it. His two arms pumped up and down with all the strength he could muster. I braced my legs against the heavy pounding of my pubis and thrust my hips forward to receive the full slam of his fists against my body.

"Man, I'm going to give this thing the workout it deserves," Blond Angel said. "Too bad it won't fit in my mouth, 'cause I'd really love to have that sex-drive juice delivered right down my throat!" He was really getting into his work, trying gamely to pull and push and slam Megameat into submission. What he wanted was a major blast of Locky Load right in his face.

I was losing control again.

"Wait a minute!" I said. "I don't think you're strong enough to get a load out of this thing."

"I sure am, stranger!" He stood pressed against my side and wrapped both hands around my long, fat prick. Then he started pounding my supercock with a force that almost threw me off my feet. "Feel good, man?" he panted. He really wanted that load in the worst way.

Blond Angel began to sweat and gasp with the exertion of beating this big piece of meat. A few shadowy revegens gathered to watch his struggle. "You'll never be able to get a load out of that thing!" said one. "You ain't man enough!"

"Yes, I am!" gasped Blond Angel.

"Here, try these!" said one of the bystanders. He produced a pair of small leather sparring gloves and slid them over Blond Angel's hands, pulling them snug and tying up the laces. He patted the Angel on the shoulder and whispered in his ear, "Go to it, baby!"

Blond Angel began to punch the underside of Megameat with a steady, slow, pounding rhythm. With each blow, my big dick would bounce back against my chest and then rebound forward to receive the next leather-clad punch. The spectators began to chant with each blow: "Come! Come! Come! Come! Come!"

I knew I was losing control of my big, loaded gonads. With each blow of the padded gloves, they bounced and caromed off my thighs. Then they began to heave in massive contractions, and I could feel hot surges through my cock's thick come tube.

Blond Angel sensed the coming eruption and positioned his body in front of my dick. Megameat was twitching uncontrollably. Suddenly thick blasts of dark chocolate lava—a pint at least—shot out and coated his chest. A Tarzan-like shout issued from my throat. The crowd cheered.

"Blond Angel wins!"

"Good show, stranger!"

Their enthusiasm deserved an encore. I decided to expend the second of the five loads Dr. Hung had pumped into me back at the Penis Enhancement Parlor.

Blond Angel was busy licking up the sweet, dark sex syrup from the swollen head of my prick when I let fly the second massive eruption. This time it was a thick white froth that resembled marshmallow syrup. My urethra burned in surging waves. The first blast hit Angel square in the middle of his face. Several minor salvos followed, which he caught in his open mouth. The crowd of revegens started to cheer again.

"The stranger is the champion! He can come at will!"

Suddenly a shadowy figure emerged from the crowd. I soon recognized him as the man with the dragon.

"Very well done, stranger!" he said. "I see you've been to see the famous Dr. Hung."

A wee fart of blue-green flame shot out from the asshole of the little leashed creature at his side. Then the revegen whispered in my ear, "But now will you defend your title as cock champion of Kama Loka?"

"You better believe I will!" I replied.

"Later, then, at the Rectum Rodeo. See you there…" He and the little dragon melted into the mist.

Now I had to find the Rectum Rodeo. I pulled my cloak tight around me and wandered off through the cool Kama Loka night, trying to make out the glowing signs. One soon emerged through the mist: RAUNCHY COMEDY PARTY.

I pulled the door open and stuck my head inside. I saw a cramped and crowded cabaret room with dirty brick walls and small candlelit tables. A brilliant white spot encircled a man on the tiny stage. His spiky platinum hair shone with reflections from his sequined lavender jumpsuit. When the crowd stopped laughing, he continued.

"I guess you don't know the difference between a faggot and a refrigerator," he told the crowd. There was a longish pregnant pause before he delivered the punch line: "A refrigerator doesn't fart when you take the meat out!"

The crowd roared. "No, but seriously…" I closed the door and continued up the Sexarcade. Signs glimmered and sparkled:

MUSEUM OF MODERN PECS!

ARENA OF ASSHOLES!

SLIME HOLE OF THE UNIVERSE!

STUDS & SLUTS REVUE!

Finally: RECTUM RODEO! I had found my next destination and, I hoped, my next adventure. I still had three of Dr. Hung's loads to go. I pulled open the rustic barn door.

The interior of the place was very much like a covered arena. There were bleachers everywhere, crowded with revegens in fancy country-and-western duds. In the sunken arena floor was a padded cockpit, about twenty feet in diameter, its floor and walls covered with black leather. In the center, under the glare of overhead lights, stood a wiry cocoa-skinned young man. His sinewy body was clad only in tight black leather bikini briefs. A murmur rose from the crowd in the bleachers as I entered.

I started hearing whisperings of "The stranger!" "Dick of death!" and "Balls of doom!"

The referee soon appeared at my side in a black-and-white striped blouse and white visor cap. "You ready to take on Chico?" he asked me, nodding toward the muscular figure standing in the padded cockpit. Chico was staring defiantly in our direction.

"You bet your ass I am!" I answered.

The ref led me into the center of the cockpit under the bright lights and spoke to the crowd.

"The stranger accepts the challenge to defend his position as cockmaster of Kama Loka!" He turned to Chico. "Do you, Chico, accept the challenge?" Chico looked my cloaked figure up and down and sneered. His sinewy muscles rippled.

"This skinny nerd is going to challenge *me*, Chico of Colón?" He snorted contemptuously. "Take off the cloak so I can laugh at your miserable white, clammy, skinny gringo body!" he snarled, showing a set of fine, glistening teeth.

With a smile I unfastened the neck clasp of my cloak and let it fall to the floor at my feet. I pulled the jockstrap to my ankles and stepped out of it to stand in the very center of the cockpit. I held my arms above my head and turned around three hundred and sixty degrees so that every spectator could have a good look. Gasps of amazement went up from the bleachers. Finally I turned to face Chico of Colón. His face went white when he gazed upon Megameat. "*Padre de Carne!*" he breathed.

The crowd was in an uproar. "Cancel the match!" shouted one spectator. "Nobody can withstand *that!*"

Another shouted, "On with the contest! We paid our UDs! Now let's see some action."

The referee turned to Chico of Colón. "What do you say, Chico? Think you can handle the challenge of Megameat?"

Chico's forehead was beaded with sweat. He swallowed hard, then he said, "I have my reputation to uphold. Yes! I accept the challenge!"

A great roar of expectation went up from the crowd, then silence as the referee raised his hand and shouted, "Gentlemen, the Rectum Rodeo presents Chico of Colón versus Megameat! Let the contest begin!" He blew two short blasts on his whistle.

The referee turned to me. "How do you want him?" he asked.

"On his stomach, with his wrists bound in front of him with leather thongs," I replied. "And put a training bit in his mouth."

From below the bleachers two attendants pushed out a big mechanical bull. On the heavy steel base of the device, a brass plaque read AUTO-BRONCO. Without either legs or head, the machine was essentially only the torso, neck, and flanks of a steed, driven up and down by powerful steel pistons. A saddle blanket was spread on the back of the Auto-Bronco, and a low English saddle with heavy-duty stirrups was cinched around the machine's belly.

Chico was stripped of his leather briefs and lifted bare-assed onto the the saddle. He lay on his stomach with his arms around the headless neck of the horse. His wrists were then tied with thick rawhide thongs. A bit was forced between his teeth, and its thick leather reins were draped across his neck. His legs dangled helplessly on either side of the bronco's wide flanks. His tan, satiny bubble butt stuck up in invitation. In challenge.

The referee held a remote control for the Auto-Bronco in his hand. "The crowd and I will decide on the speed of the bucking. You have to maintain penetration and stay astride Chico's buns, or you lose. Now, stranger, you want it dry or greased-up?"

"Give it a good shot of bacon drippings," I replied.

One of the attendants began to slather Chico's bung hole with thick, grayish fat. He worked some of the salty grease into the sphincter ring with three fingers. "*Ay, ay, ay!*" moaned Chico as the salt penetrated the delicate membranes of his anal canal. "*Madre de Manteca!*"

The lights on the bleachers dimmed and went out, leaving the spectators in darkness. Several more overhead lights brightened over the cockpit. I strode over and stepped up on the base of the Auto-Bronco. My half-hard supercock was slowly growing to its full length and girth at the thought of plunging into Chico's hot, salty, pink puckered anus.

"No-o-o!" came a high-pitched scream from the bleachers. "My darling Chico! He can never survive this contest! Release my Chico from his contract. Have mercy!"

"Shut up!" came a chorus of voices.

A deep hush fell on the arena, broken only by the muffled sobs of Chico's admirer. I began my penetration with the skill of a surgeon and the gentle firmness of a pony trainer. I placed the huge cherry-red turret of Megameat against the bastion of Chico's tight little sphincter. I felt the body-warm bacon grease begin to slide around the circumference of the dick head as it began to force the opening wider.

Chico began to moan loudly as Megameat began its slow, inexorable penetration, the tissues of Chico's anus spreading apart with each new invasion. The bright red color of my cock head seemed to glow like a hot poker in the overhead glare. I could hear the audience breathing softly in anticipation. Under my firm pressure—but very slowly, tiny bit by tiny bit—Chico's bung hole began to soften and relax. The bacon grease felt hot and slightly gritty.

The referee was watching closely, his face just inches away from the center of the action. Chico was beginning to squirm under the onslaught. I had to be careful and not lose penetration, or I would forfeit the contest. Chico's squirming was increasing, threatening to expel the huge intruder. I leaned forward and placed my hands on his shoulders, pushing him down firmly against the saddle. He grew a bit quieter. I leaned over and growled in his ear, "Lie still, damn it, or I'll drive it in all at once!"

"No! Please!" he moaned. "I'll try!"

The salty fat was beginning to make my dick tingle. I forced the big red dick head forward a quarter-inch more and felt with satisfaction that it was starting to work its way in. Then I began to meet more resistance. I leaned over Chico's muscular back and breathed in his ear, "Open up or else! I'm not kidding!" The bacon grease was beginning to send up the faint aroma of frying.

He pleaded, "It hurts bad, señor! Take it easy on Chico's butt. Please!" He tried to squirm away again, but it was too late. The big cherry-red head was now past the point of no return, and his movements served only to send it farther up his straining rectum. I straightened up to watch the beautiful sight of my dick head slowly disappearing into the stretched orifice.

Chico of Colón's head jerked back in agony and ecstasy as the colorful intruder slid fully into his dark bung hole. "*Aie-e-e!*" he screamed.

The referee blew a short blast on his whistle. "The dick head is in!" he shouted. The crowd yelled its approval. "Fuck him good, stranger!" someone yelled. A deeper voice grunted, "Show that cocky little bastard who's boss!"

I waited a few moments to let Chico settle down. His moaning gradually subsided as his tight rectum formed itself around its huge new occupying force. The ref produced a Kama Loka ruler from his pocket and proceeded to take measurements.

"From sphincter to hilt, thirteen inches to go," he shouted to the crowd. There was a gasp of disbelief, then anxious silence. Now I had truly gained entry into the hallowed precincts of Chico's lithe, brown body, and the real action could begin. I looked down at the beautiful sight of the enormous alabaster shaft of Megameat glowing in the bright light of the arena. The thick blue veins were pulsing with energy down to the jet-black curly hair at the base. The cherry-red head could not be seen at all; it was securely locked in place by Chico's tight, contracted sphincter.

Thirteen inches of rock-hard Megameat waited, glistening, under the overhead glare. Now I felt like entertaining the crowd. A bit of simple arithmetic gave me this: I would push into Chico's hot ass exactly one-half inch at a time. Complete penetration would thus take twenty-six thrusts.

"Referee! Mark off Megameat in half-inch sections," I demanded. The agile ref, using a thick black marker, quickly sectioned off twenty-six intervals along the engorged shaft.

"Count down the alphabet!" I shouted to the crowd. "A!"

"A!" roared the crowd.

"A is for *anus*!" I shouted. "The anus I'm stretching wide." And with that, I shoved in the first half inch of rock-hard dick shaft. Chico moaned, "*Ayyy, padre!*"

"B!" screamed the crowd.

"B is for *balls*! Fat, loaded balls of doom!"

With that, I forced in the second half inch of Megameat. Chico gasped and gurgled.

"C!" yelled the crowd.

"C is for *cock*! Big, big, *big* cock!" I pushed into the rectum the third half inch.

"*Gmmmppphhh!*" came from Chico's throat.

"D!"

"D is for *dong*! D is for *deeper*!" I shoved my dong deeper by a half inch. Chico writhed and squirmed.

"E!"

"E is for *erection!*" Another half inch of erection disappeared into Chico's bung hole.

"F!" shouted the crowd.

"F is for *fucking!*" I responded with another half-inch shove.

"G!" screamed the spectators.

"G is for *gonads!*" I slammed in another half inch.

"H!"

I grinned as I said, "H is for *helpless!*" I drove Megameat deeper into Chico's helpless rectum.

"I!" yelled the crowd.

"I is for *injection,* and J is for *jism!*" I yelled as I shoved a full inch deeper. Chico screamed, and so did the spectators.

"K!"

I thought for a moment before I replied. "K is for *Kama Loka,* City of Desire!" I drove in another half inch. The crowd began waving pennants reading KAMA LOKA FUCKFEST.

"L!" they yelled. "L!"

"L is for *load*—a big, big, *big* load, coming up soon!" I replied as I pushed another half-inch deeper. Chico was moaning and writhing under the intense pressure from Megameat.

"M!" screamed the spectators.

"M is for *Megameat!*" I answered, driving in another half inch.

The referee blew his whistle and raised his arms for silence. "It's halfway in! Megameat is halfway in!" he yelled to the crowd. The bleachers erupted in a frenzy of applause and cheering. The referee took a measurement. "Still six-and-a-half inches to go!" he announced.

Chico groaned and shuddered, "No...please...have mercy! My asshole can't take anymore!"

The referee was adamant. "You agreed to the contest, Chico," he said, "now, take it like a man. Or are you a *cabrón?*"

"Chico of Colón is no *cabrón!*" he gasped defiantly. His sinewy back was glistening with sweat, the gluteus muscles in his tight buns twitching uncontrollably. I felt his tortured guts contracting in waves against the shaft of my huge cock. I wanted to shove it all in at once, right away, but I knew that I had to be patient. One-half inch at a time. Slow and easy.

"Let the contest resume," said the ref. He blew two short blasts on his whistle. I looked down at the tortured red ring of Chico's anus wrapped around the massive girth of Megameat. Little flecks of bacon grease sparkled around the edges of his asshole, and some thin brownish ass juice dribbled down the backs of his thighs.

I reached forward and grabbed the reins of Chico's bridle in my right fist and pulled the bit tight against his teeth. Then I carefully put my feet into the stirrups of the saddle and poised my full weight over his body. "Please go easy on Chico!" he moaned through his clenched teeth.

I took a deep breath and yelled, "N!"

"N!" screamed the crowd.

"N is for *nuts*! Big, loaded nuts!" My big nuts bounced against Chico's spread thighs as I pushed another half inch of fat dick into his bung hole. I could hear his teeth grating against the metal bit between his jaws. I pulled the reins and yanked his head back. He whinnied like a pony.

"O!" yelled the crowd.

"O is for *organ*, huge organ of death. O is for *orgasm*. O is for *orgy*!" I shoved another half inch of the organ of death into his rectum as I yanked back on the reins.

"P!" screamed the crowd.

"P is for *prick*! Thick, thick, *thick* prick!" An additional half inch of thick dick slid into the straining orifice.

"Q!" the crowd shouted.

"Q is for *queer*! *Cabrón! Mariposa!*" I said to Chico. "His queer ass is a cunt hole for a real man's dick." I plowed a thick half inch of man dick into his guts.

He shuddered and shook. "Chico is no *mariposa*!" he gasped.

The countdown continued. "R!" the crowd yelled.

"R is for *rectum*!" I said. "Rectum Rodeo, home of the fuck-fest!" The crowd cheered as I drove another half inch of Megameat into Chico's brown ass.

"S!" the spectators yelled.

"S is for *screw*," I answered, flexing my legs in the stirrups and screwing forward with an additional half inch of thick meat.

"T!" shouted the crowd.

"T is for *testicles*. Tight, turgid, tumescent, terrible, threatening testicles of doom!" They rebounded against Chico's legs as I drove in another half-inch quota of dick shaft.

"U!" yelled the crowd.

"U is for...for..." I couldn't think of one.

Chico's breathy voice said, "Let me count now, Mr. Megameat. U is for *unload*, like when you unload your big testicles of doom into Chico's guts. Give me the next half inch!" I shoved another measure into the helpless asshole.

The crowd had now quieted down to hear Chico's low, moaning voice. The referee watched closely. "Still five sections to go—two-and-a-half inches!" he yelled.

I heard whispers from the bleachers: "He'll never make it... he's at the end of his rope."

Chico's moaning voice continued. "V! V is for *vagina*, my pussy-ass man-hole vagina that needs another half inch of monster meat!" I complied with a thrust of my hips. "W is for *wimp*!" Chico went on. "W is for *wad*! This little wimp needs a big wad of man juice up his ass, señor!" I pushed against Chico's buns with a further measure of dick.

"One-and-a-half inches to go!" shouted the ref.

Chico's voice was growing weaker. I leaned forward to hear his faint words, putting my cheek against his. "Oh, señor, I have never felt such a thing as this!" he moaned softly. "My whole body is filled up with your great prick! I love you. I love you. Take me to heaven, señor!" He seemed to be regaining strength.

"X!" he moaned. "X is for *x-tasy*! Now and forever!" Another half inch of dick disappeared. "Y is for *yell*!" He opened his mouth and let out a gurgling yell as I drove in the penultimate half inch of cock.

"Z is for *zero*, nothing, all done, the end!" I shouted triumphantly as I slammed in the last bit of rock-hard thick cock.

Chico moaned, shuddered, and lay still. My chest, plastered with sweat, rested against his muscular back. My straining legs relaxed in the stirrups.

There was silence in the arena. You could hear a pin drop. I could feel the intense sensations of Megameat throbbing and pulsing hotly, buried to the hilt, deep in Chico's body. His steamy guts answered with soft, peristaltic contractions against the thick, rigid intruder. After a few minutes of awed, respectful silence, someone began to clap. Soon there was general applause as the audience rose to its feet. Chico and I lay glued together as one body. Under the applause, I alone could hear his soft breathing as he repeated over and over, "I love you... I love you... Fill me up..." Perhaps he was delirious.

The applause dwindled, and the crowd sat down. Someone yelled, "Start the Auto-Bronco!" Another shouted, "Let's see some real fucking!"

The referee blew a short blast on his whistle and proclaimed, "Starting Auto-Bronco!" He fiddled with the remote control. I felt the body of our steed begin to rise slowly into the air on its motor-driven leg pistons. It rose slowly about two feet and then began to descend until it hit the bottom of its course with a small jolt, which sent shivers through our bodies. Then it began to rise again slowly. Then descend again. Again that excruciating jolt, which seemed to drive my huge, swollen dick still farther into Chico's guts. "Fuck me hard, señor!" he moaned. "My *mariposa* vagina ass needs to be fucked real hard!"

The Auto-Bronco rose, fell, and jolted over and over again. Each jolt was exquisite torture for both me and Chico. "Start the roll!" yelled someone from the bleachers. "Yeah, start the roll. Let's see if he can stay on!"

The referee blew a short blast on his whistle. "Starting roll movement. Watch yourself, stranger! Don't get unhorsed, or you'll lose the contest." He punched several more buttons on the remote, and soon I felt the Auto-Bronco begin to roll from side to side, about a foot in each direction, while it continued its up-and-down movement.

131

The rolling movement was causing the full length of Megameat to grind and torque against the straining walls of Chico's intestines. *"Padre!"* he gasped.

I raised my body up so that I could carry my weight on the stirrups. I grasped the reins firmly in both hands. My big, thick dick was still buried in Chico's butt hole, where it seemed to be held by some kind of suction. My loaded nuts bounced against the backside of the bronco. "Faster, faster!" yelled the crowd. The referee turned up the speed.

The Auto-Bronco began to lunge up and down about once every second. The jolt when it hit bottom jarred my teeth and slammed my Megameat mercilessly into Chico's anus. The suction in his rectum started to release after a few dozen of these jolts, and after several more slams my cock began to slide in and out of his slimy bung hole like a thick white piston. The shaft was covered with steaming bacon fat and sticky ass juice. The sensation was indescribable as my full fifteen inches of man dick slid in and out of Chico's hot, tight rectum. He moaned and squirmed with agony. "Fuck my *cabrón* cunt hole real good, Mr. Megameat. I love you!"

"Faster, faster!" screamed the crowd. The ref upped the speed to twice a second. Now Megameat was withdrawing almost its full length before slamming back down deep into Chico's butt. Groans of ecstasy and gasps of pain issued from his throat. The crowd was insatiable. I noticed spectators in the front rows taking out their dicks and whacking vigorously. "Fuck him harder!" they roared. "Start the pitch! Start the pitch!"

The referee adjusted the remote control. Suddenly the Auto-Bronco began to lurch forward and backward as well as up and down and side to side. I was in a withdrawal movement from Chico's asshole, and I almost lost my balance and flew forward. I recovered my stance and tightened my thighs against the sides of the machine. I grabbed the front rim of the saddle in my left hand. The Auto-Bronco lurched in wild bucking movements as my body alternately flew forward and backward. My huge dick drove in and out of Chico's slimy ass.

"Ride that ass, stranger!" a voice in the crowd urged. "Fuck him good!"

The slapping of my huge gonads against the Auto-Bronco soon brought me past the point of no return. As the big, thick dick shaft ground up and down through the slimy bacon fat, I felt surges of hot love juice start to squirt out into Chico's entrails. My balls were contracting with each jolt of the machine and sending wave upon wave of lavalike spume into the helpless body. "*Ggau-u-ughhh!*" he gasped. His intestinal tract had filled up completely, and gobs of sticky white sex syrup started to pour out of his mouth and run down the sides of the Auto-Bronco. My meat continued to slam into his body with each wild jolt of the powerful pistons. More thick marshmallowlike spunk surged out of his mouth between his teeth, clenched around the bit.

The bleachers went into a wild frenzy at the sight of the white spunk. Dozens of ecstatic groans erupted as gobs of milky white come started flying around the arena, catching some spectators in the face as they whacked their swollen pricks. "Come! Come! Come!" they chanted. Showers of white erupted.

The referee backed off the remote speed control, and the Auto-Bronco slowed down. The spectators sighed in satisfaction. The machine ground slowly to a halt. There was a long silence broken only by heavy postorgasmic breathing. I fell forward against Chico's sweaty back, gulping air into my lungs. Megameat still throbbed and burned inside the ravaged butt hole of my challenger.

The arena attendants grabbed me under the armpits and slowly lifted me off Chico's quiet body. As they did so, Megameat slowly slid out until, with a slurping sound, the cherry-red head appeared for the first time since the start of the contest. Chico's empty guts sighed out a long, gassy, postfuck fart, smelling of frying bacon. I was exhausted, but I managed to stand up when the attendants set me on my feet on the floor of the cockpit.

Chico was not so lucky. They untied his hands and laid him face up on a stretcher. He didn't move very much; he just breathed softly and murmured under his breath, "*Te amo. Te amo.*" I still had two of Dr. Hung's loads to go, so I strode over to the stretcher and stood over Chico's supine body. I grabbed my still-erect cock in both hands and began to milk it up and down. My huge nuts contracted again as I felt surges of hot fluid well up. Soon spurts of dark chocolate sex syrup sprayed out of the cherry-red head and coated Chico's body from head to toe. Furious applause rang out from the bleachers.

"What a guy!" someone yelled. "What a dick!" yelled another. "Best show I've ever seen at the Rectum Rodeo!"

The referee raised my right hand into the air and shouted, "Champion Megameat!" He handed me a gleaming trophy in the shape of two golden gonads. He placed my cloak over my shoulders. The crowd yelled and screamed.

The house lights went up, and the spectators started to disperse. The man with the dragon appeared out of the crowd. "Great show!" he said, patting me on the back.

"I guess the party's over," I said as I watched the crowd disappear into the misty night. "Time for me to be going home..."

"You can't leave yet," he said. "You still have one load left to go. Didn't Dr. Hung pump five loads into your gonads?"

"Yes," I answered. "I guess he did."

"Well, you can't take it with you. You have to leave it in Kama Loka. Time to pay up." He got down on his knees and thrust his head into the folds of my cloak. He fastened his lips on the head of my still-tumescent prick. He began to massage the shaft with both hands. The little dragon shuffled around behind me and started darting his hot, spiky tongue into my asshole.

"He thinks he's human," explained the revegen. He continued to massage my cock. I felt my nuts start to heave and contract.

"Time to get...up," he seemed to be saying. My nuts were burning.

"Time to get up. Wake up!" I opened my eyes to see Dr. Wünder's face in the dim light. My nuts were bursting, and I could feel sticky spurts of come inside my Jockey shorts.

Dr. Wünder strode over to the window of his office and pulled open the thick drapes. The pale gray light of dawn filled the room. He sat down in the chair next to the divan. His eyes seemed to flash a mischievous sparkle. "Kama Loka must have been fun," he said, smiling.

"It sure was," I replied. "When can I go again?"

"How about tonight?" said Dr. Wünder.

PART THREE

"So, Ted, your first visit to Kama Loka was full of sexual adventure?" Dr. Wünder asked, smiling knowingly.

"Yes," I replied sheepishly. I knew I was blushing. I hadn't dared to tell Dr. Wünder the full story of my outrageous experiences in Kama Loka. I had awakened from my previous evening of lucid dreaming with my shorts sticky with semen. I spent the entire day anticipating this evening, unable to concentrate on my classes at Saratoga University. Now it was time to enter the lucid dream state again under the guidance of Dr. Wünder and his Lucid Dream Monitor.

"Well," Dr. Wünder said, "I understand your reluctance to relate your adventures in their entirety. Perhaps when we get to know each other a little better, you will be willing to make a full report. In the meantime, let's continue with our research. Just relax and enjoy your lucid dream time in Kama Loka tonight. Direct the dream in any way you like. Perhaps some information or insight will appear unexpectedly."

Dr. Wünder came around the desk. As he stood, I could catch the sharp outline of his heavy cock through his trousers. He put his hand on my shoulder paternally. "Ready for another dream voyage?" he asked.

"Absolutely!" I replied with enthusiasm. I had been anticipating this moment all day. I stood and followed Dr. Wünder over to the large divan on the opposite side of the office. As I reclined, he pulled the heavy drapes over the windows. I slipped on the goggles and gloves that were attached to the dream monitor.

Dr. Wünder handed me a small glass filled with pale pink liquid. "Here's your acetylcholine, Ted. Drink up!" I downed the glass in one gulp. Last night's dose had worked only too well, sending me into a deep dream state for over eight hours of lucid nonstop sexual fantasy.

The dream monitor hummed a musical tone. I closed my eyes and waited for the tingle from the goggles, alerting me that I was in the REM dream state. "Relax and enjoy your time in Kama Loka," Dr. Wünder repeated. My body was completely relaxed and yet alert. I crossed my hands across my stomach and moved my gloved fingers to type a message to the dream monitor: *See you in the morning, Dr. Wünder.*

His voice seemed far away as he intoned, "Relax and enjoy yourself in Kama Loka—Dream City of Desire!" The goggles gave a short tingle against my eyes. I looked overhead at the neon letters glowing against the misty night sky: WELCOME TO KAMA LOKA.

I was dreaming. I was lucid. I was again in Kama Loka.

I looked down at my body. I was dressed in worn Levi's and a red T-shirt with black letters on the front reading WILL ACCEPT MERCY FUCK. I felt my cock through the worn denim…my normal, nerdy, grad-student cock. The magnificent fifteen-inch Megameat of last night was gone. Maybe I would have to find Dr. Hung Soo Fat again.

I began to walk through the cool night mist of Kama Loka. I might well spend the entire night looking for the Penis Enhancement Parlor. Nothing seemed to stay in the same place. I needed transportation. I concentrated on directing the dream. I heard a toot behind me and turned to see a deep purple taxi glide up to my side. The driver stuck his head out the window. It was the man with the dragon from last night. The little dragon sat in the seat beside the driver, twitching its tail.

"Need a lift?" he asked. "Get in!"

The taxi interior matched the exterior paint job, with purple satin upholstery and soft lavender carpeting. I sank into the overstuffed seat.

"Where to, stranger?" asked the revegen.

Good question. My mind was racing. Should I see Dr. Hung and have my cock enhanced again? What about Teddy the Bear? Maybe the Temple of Priapus? I had noticed so many attractions last night. Kama Loka was most likely inexhaustible.

"Just drive," I said. "Show me the town."

"How about a little tour of Fantasy Lane?" asked the driver. "We're almost there now." Colored signs glowed through the mist. My tour guide turned down a narrow street. "Anything strikes your fancy, just let me know." The purple taxi glided slowly over gaudy zigzag reflections on the damp pavement.

On my left I saw the words UFO ABDUCTION printed in weird green letters. "What's that about?" I asked.

"Well, that's where you get picked up and transported to a flying saucer, then scientifically examined and sexually abused by aliens who are doing research on human sexuality. Very exciting…in a weird way. Haven't tried it myself yet."

Then I spotted RUBBER RUMPUS ROOM. "And that one?" I asked.

"There you get fitted with a skintight suit of thin synthetic rubber—very stretchy, very clingy, very sensual. Your choice of color—black being the most popular. Your head is encased in something like a gas mask with clear eye lenses. The suit has strategic zippers so various parts of the body can be accessed, such as the nipples and the penis and testicles. Two extremely aggressive studs, also in rubber, work you over with various erotic techniques."

My cock was beginning to harden inside my jeans. "Like what kind of techniques?" I asked.

"Oh, you know, anything that causes the rubber to cling or rub over sensitive body parts—and slapping, pulling, and snapping the rubber. My favorite is where they tie you up with big rubber straps and wet you down with high-pressure water hoses. The sensation when the jets of water play over your rubber-covered body is unbelievable, especially on the cock and balls, which are stretched out and pummeled until you finally shoot a hot load of jism inside the sweaty rubber."

By now my cock was fully hard, and I was rubbing it through the crotch of my jeans. I was definitely ready for one of the attractions in Fantasy Lane. "What's that one about?" I asked, pointing to the sign reading ENGLISH SCHOOL DAYS.

"The instructors at the school are extremely picky. Any tiny infringement of the rules is answered with corporal punishment.

If your shoes aren't shined properly, you may be made to drop your pants and shorts in front of the class. You'll be forced to bend over a desk while the instructor flogs your bare ass unmercifully. Depending on his mood, he may use a cane or a belt or maybe a riding crop. Your genitals are hanging down over the edge of the desk, and some of the strokes of the whip land on the underside of your unprotected cock and balls. If you get a hard-on, then the instructor gets really mad and lays into your butt until it's flaming red. Sometimes you'll shoot your load as he paddles your buns, and the come runs down the side of the desk for everyone to see."

My cock was throbbing with excitement. I unbuttoned my jeans and pulled out my dick and balls, slowly stroking up and down the rigid shaft.

My guide looked at me in the rearview mirror, smiling. The purple taxi cruised slowly down Fantasy Lane. "How about this one?" the revegen asked. I looked to my right to see VARSITY LOCKER ROOM. "Sound appealing?"

"What happens in there?" I asked. I slid my hand slowly along the length of my throbbing dick.

"It's after football practice. The regular head coach is away, so the players know they can get away with fooling around. All the big guys are proud of their powerful physiques, broad shoulders, hairy chests, massive thighs and calves, and, last but not least, their heavy-duty dicks swinging between their legs. The tiled shower room is filled with steam from all the showerheads spraying hot water. You're not on the team. You're one of the cheerleaders. You find an excuse to take a shower at the same time as the big guys so you can stare at their huge equipment with boyish envy. They're all taking their time, soaping their big flaccid organs, making lots of white lather as they stroke and pull. One guy snaps his washcloth at your ass, and they all laugh when you jump. Murphy, the fullback, gets fully hard first. He's really proud of his long, thick pole. It stands up to his navel. Then the other players start to get full erections. 'Come over here and play with my dick, nerd!' Murphy says to you. You have no choice but to obey. You kneel in front of Murphy's big come cannon and work up a lather of soapsuds. Using both hands, you start to massage the fullback's stiff, meaty cock. You massage and pull on his huge nuts. The rest of the team is standing around in a circle, watching the action, all pulling on their pricks. Murphy's hips start to thrust forward in preorgasmic tension. 'Mmm!' he groans. His come-loaded cock twitches and turns beet-red under the expert jacking-off you're administering. 'Me next!' says Kowalski, the tackle. You give a few more heavy jerks, and Murphy's straining dick unleashes a series of hot sperm blasts right in your face. The next big stud, Kowalski, steps up to take his place. 'Work on that big dick, nerd!' he commands. Your arms are tired, and your knees ache from pressing against the bare wet tile, but you need to feel those hot blasts of sperm in your face, so you start to massage the thick, fleshy Polish sausage throbbing in front of you. Larsen, the quarterback, yells, 'Me next!'"

My poor cock was throbbing like crazy. "What happens then?" I gasped.

"You get to jerk off the whole team, unless one of the guys maybe decides to shove his big dick in your mouth or up your ass," replied the driver. The purple taxi glided on through the misty night.

"What's that one?" I asked, my sweaty palm massaging my excited cock. I was looking at a sign reading INTERROGATION CHAMBER in red neon against black.

"While on a reconnaissance mission, you've been captured behind enemy lines. You've burned all the identification papers in the pockets of your uniform. Your interrogation takes place in a bare concrete room containing only a couple of steel lockers. You're sitting on a plain wooden chair. A spot bulb over your head leaves the rest of the room in shadow. Your interrogator enters, wearing a simple khaki uniform and a black mask over his face. He is a big, powerfully built man with a massive bulge in the crotch of his trousers. He makes you give him a urine sample in a glass jar—part of your 'medical profile'. He makes a disparaging comment about your small dick. 'Do all American spies

have such little dicks?' he wants to know. You protest that you
are not a spy but a pilot who crashed behind enemy lines. He
does not believe your story. He has no choice but to restrain you,
since you may be dangerous. He ties your hands to the chair
rungs behind you with strong Manila rope. Your ankles are tightly bound to the back legs of the chair so that your knees are
spread and your crotch is exposed. The spotlight is turned
brighter in your face."

I was pulling faster on my superhard dick. "Then what?"

"You refuse to give him any information as to your mission. He
is forced to use stronger methods. You know he is excited by his
power over you because you can see the outline of his erect prick
through the khaki of his tight uniform. He opens one of the lockers and removes a large black metal case. He places the case by
your feet and opens the lid. Inside is a heavy-duty electrical-stor-
age battery. He pulls out some wires fitted with alligator clips. He
grabs the collar of your uniform in his big fists and rips open the
front of your shirt. You hear the ping of the buttons as they hit
the bare concrete floor. He attaches a clip to each of your nipples. The metal bites into your tender flesh, and you groan. He
wonders whether all American spies are such little-dicked sissies.
He massages his hard cock through the cloth of his trousers. 'Tell
me about your mission,' he demands as he sends the first low jolt
of electricity into your tender nipples. Your chest and stomach
muscles contract in agony, your spine arches, and you strain
against the heavy ropes cutting into your arms and ankles. A
scream of pain issues from your throat. You still refuse to talk. He
turns up the juice and delivers another electric jolt to your burning tits. After a dozen or more of these agonizing bursts of current, you begin to lose track of time. Your helpless body is wet
with perspiration, saturating your pants and what is left of your
torn shirt. You are almost unconscious, and your head lolls on
your chest. Your hair hangs in your face, limp with sweat."

"Don't stop...go on!" I implored.

"He grabs your hair and pulls your head back. Then he slaps
you across the face twice, once on each side—hard. You wake up

141

fast. You feel a trickle of blood run down your chin. You see that the interrogator's dick is really hard now, stretching from his crotch up toward the waistband of his trousers. 'You sadistic bastard!' you shout at him, but you can't help staring at the big, hard dick just inches from your face. You lick the blood from your lips. He wants to know if all American spies are sissy faggots, because he knows you've been staring at his big bulge. He runs the fingers of his right hand over the full length of his erection. He does this several times, watching you watch him. Then he unbuckles the belt of your trousers, grabbing the waistband of your pants with both hands and pulling. The fabric and the zipper rip apart. He yanks the elastic waistband of your Jockey shorts until it tears with a snap. He rips the rest of your shorts away until your genitals are exposed. He attaches two alligator clips to your balls and then two to the soft tissue below the head of your cock. He says he's going to fry your faggot American cock. You wince with pain as the clips bite into your flesh."

"Yes...what then?" I leaned back into the purple cushions, whacking away at my throbbing dick.

"The interrogator says you have one last chance before he jolts your dick and roasts your balls. Tell him what he wants to know about your spy mission and save yourself a lot of unnecessary pain, he says. He is massaging his dick through his khaki trousers as he threatens you. You see a wet spot soaking through the cloth near the head of his dick. He is incredibly excited to have another man completely in his power, helpless, bound with thick, heavy rope. You shake your head from side to side. No, you say, you won't talk, even though he does his worst to your genitals with his electric stunner. You yell at him, telling him he's a sick monster. This gets him more excited than ever, so he slaps you across the face again. Then he reaches for the rheostat to bring up the electricity to your helpless genitals."

"Then what happens?"

The revegen taxi driver leaned back over the driver's seat and watched me yank on my dick. The vehicle glided by itself through the Kama Loka night.

"Is that the way you beat your meat?" he demanded. "You're a rank amateur. You need a lot of help! And soon!" He grabbed the wheel and turned the taxi sharply to the right. Moments later he pulled up in front of an ivy-covered building. The sign on the facade in brass letters read KAMA LOKA ACADEMY OF MASTURBATORY ARTS. "Go in there and take some classes," he advised. "You won't regret it."

I buttoned up my jeans and got out of the taxi. I reached into my pockets looking for Kama Loka money—units of desire. Nothing! The driver laughed and tossed me a small velvet drawstring bag. It was full of little gold UDs. He drove away into the misty night. I heard his voice from a distance: "What's real?"

I climbed the forbidding stone stairs of the Academy of Masturbatory Arts and pulled open the front door. The brass handle was shaped like a big, erect phallus held by a fist. I walked along a dim corridor, my footsteps echoing.

"Can I be of assistance?" a voice behind me asked. I turned to see a heavyset man wearing a plaid vest and puffing on a pipe.

"Uh...is there someone in charge?" I began hesitantly. "I want to find out about taking some classes."

"You may talk to me," the man answered. "I'm the director of the academy, Master Bates. Come into the consultation room."

I followed Master Bates through an open door and into a large paneled room with a desk and several chairs. He took a seat behind the desk and motioned for me to take an empty chair. He placed his elbows on the desktop and put the tips of his fingers together.

"Now, what can I do for you?" he said.

"I think I need some masturbation classes, Master Bates. My technique is very amateurish."

The director looked at me gravely over the tips of his fingers. Then he reached into a top drawer and produced a paper-bound brochure. "Here is the catalog of our classes for this term," he said. "Why don't you look it over and see if anything appeals to you. In the meantime, I'll check our enrollment situation and see if we can fit you in."

I studied the catalog. The cover showed a picture of the ivy-covered building with the name of the school in gold type: KAMA LOKA ACADEMY OF MASTURBATORY ARTS. Beneath that was the slogan KLAMA BEATS THEM ALL! The school's logo was a fist holding an erect cock. I opened the catalog and began to read the course offerings:

Channel 1–"History of Masturbation." Ever since man learned to walk upright, freeing his hands for masturbation, the human race has spilled trillions of gallons of sperm upon the earth. Explore the thrilling techniques of the ancient Sumerians, Egyptians, and Incas. Study the horseback methods of Genghis Khan's Golden Horde, the penis suspension of the Apaches, the blubber banging of the Inuit tribes, and much more.

Channel 2–"Metaphysics of Orgasm." What is orgasm, and why is it so wonderful? How does it fit into the larger scheme of things? Is orgasm a cosmic principle or merely a physical sensation? Explore these and other fascinating topics, which will help to deepen your appreciation of orgasm. Recommended reading: *The Sexy Universe* by Constantine Jakinoff, Ph.D.

Channel 3–"Lubricants for Masturbation." A hands-on class that introduces you to an enormous range of possible materials, each with its own special effects. Experiment with both man-made and natural greases, oils, jellies, ointments, and slimes. (Materials are provided.)

Channel 4–"Jacking Off in Public Places." You can have an orgasm anytime and anyplace you like! These newly developed secret underhanded techniques allow you to masturbate in crowded movie theaters, restaurants, buses, supermarkets, or churches. (Fieldwork may be required.)

Channel 5–"Visual Aids for Masturbation." Learn to increase your fantasy potential through careful selection of pornographic materials. Surveys artwork, magazines, photographs, stories, videotapes, and CD-ROMs. Have fun making your own porn!

Channel 6–"Electromechanical Stimulation." Discover unique methods for modern masturbation! New devices, unavailable until recently, expand the boundaries of self-abuse. Enjoy commonplace devices perverted for autoerotic use—vacuum cleaners, bilge pumps, vibrating sanders, electric drills, massagers, reciprocating handsaws, milking machines, etc. A course for the adventurous! (Materials provided.)

Channel 7—"Mahalinga Yoga." Practice the ancient Hindu discipline of the Great Lingam of Shiva. Exotic, centuries-old techniques will show you how to stretch, engorge, and thicken your phallus permanently. Discover the Way of Sperm Retention (orgasm without ejaculation) and the resulting hormonal benefits for the entire body.

Channel 8—"Unendurable Pleasure Indefinitely Prolonged." A class for the advanced student, based on the study of the ancient Taoist scripture *The Scroll of the Hidden Rosebud.* Not for the faint of heart.

Channel 9—"Frontiers of Masturbation." Toward what forms and techniques will solo sex evolve in the next millennium? Weightlessness, genetic engineering, virtual reality, and cybersex are opening astonishing new vistas for the serious student of onanistic delight.

I looked up from the catalog. Master Bates was staring at me expectantly. "Well, have you decided?" he asked.

"They all sound so...so stimulating," I responded. "What do the channel numbers mean?"

Master Bates rose from his desk. "Let me show you your masturbation module, and things will become clearer." He led the way down the corridor and opened a door marked #57. We entered a small room perhaps ten feet square. I noted a reclining chair, a wooden stool, a towel rack with many clean white towels, a small refrigerator, and a large upright metal locker. Set in the wall opposite the recliner was a giant video screen. A large mirror filled the rest of the wall.

"Your instructors will speak and demonstrate on the video screen. Use the channel selector built into the arm of the recliner to change the program. You see, we at KLAMA believe that masturbation is a solitary art best practiced in private. In fact, one of our primary rules at the academy is that the students must not touch one another. Anyone violating this rule will face immediate expulsion. Is that clear?" Master Bates looked stern.

"Yes, yes, I understand. No touching except myself."

"And remember," he cautioned, "try not to ejaculate."

"OK, I'll remember. No shooting my load."

Master Bates smiled in satisfaction. He opened the door of the locker to reveal a bewildering assortment of objects, boxes, jars, wires, tubes. "Any materials you may need are in the locker," he said, "and feel free to help yourself to anything in the refrigerator if you want a snack." He started toward the door, then stopped. "Oh, just one more little thing," he said. "The tuition."

"Tuition?" I pulled out the little bag of gold UDs and handed it to Master Bates. "Is this enough?" I asked.

He hefted the bag in his palm, not bothering to open it. "I'm sure it will be quite sufficient," he responded. "Enjoy your classes, and if you need me for any reason, you can reach me on Channel 12. Until we *meat* again, happy whacking!" He grinned at me mischievously as he closed the door behind him.

I was alone in the masturbation module, and my dick was twitching in anticipation. I quickly removed my jeans and shirt. I spread a big white towel over the lounge and lay back, stark naked. I could see the reflection of my entire body in the mirror next to the screen. I looked up. The ceiling was mirrored as well. My dick was standing straight up, begging for attention. I was in the mood for a good, heavy, long session of creative self-abuse. I pushed the ON button on the remote control. The video screen flashed to life.

On Channel 1, the "History of Masturbation" course was already in progress: A horde of Mongolian warriors gallops across the steppes of central Asia under a deep blue sky. "The warriors of Genghis Khan relieved the tedium of long hours on horseback with the use of the Mongolian cock harness," the voice-over narration explains. Close-up of a young warrior, his fur jacket and cap and long mustache blowing in the wind. "The Mongolian harness provided hours of intense sexual stimulation caused by the movement of the horse." Close-up of the semierect penis of the young warrior dangling against the saddle from the open front of his soft leather trousers. He yanks his long, fat yellow dick outward and upward and then begins to wrap a long, wide leather thong around the base of his cock and balls. "Notice that the harness starts at the center part of the thong, which is about one meter long." He completely encircles the base of the testicles and cock shaft several times with the leather, pulling it tight as he wraps. He draws his two gonads against the shaft of his cock so that one is on each side. Then he wraps again several turns up his cock, pulling firmly each time so as to make one single package of the nuts and cock. The veins are standing out on the shaft. He uses the ends of the leather thong like a shoelace, winding around the long shaft in opposing spirals. Now he is above the tightly bound gonads. When he reaches the head of the cock, he makes a secure double turn and then a slipknot. "The cock and balls are now completely wrapped in leather, and the top knot is secure." Holding the rest of the leather thong, he pulls his cock-ball package down against the leather of the saddle and secures the end to a small iron ring attached to the front of the saddle. Now his cock and balls are rubbing against the saddle. The horse starts to move, and the camera tracks along. His cock and balls are bouncing upward, then slapping down against the hard leather saddle.

"Riding for hours or even days with the Mongolian harness in place produced a state of constant sexual arousal," the narrator continues. "The warrior prided himself on being able to resist orgasm for long periods of time. It is likely that the bloodthirsty brutality of the Mongol warrior was due in great part to the use of this device, which produced huge amounts of testosterone."

The camera shows several close-ups of husky warriors galloping across the plains, their big, tough Mongol cock meat stretching, lifting, bouncing, and slapping as they ride. In the distance is a small village of sheepherders. They spot the Mongol horde advancing toward them and begin to run in all directions. Too late! The horde is upon them in moments. A muscular young

ERNEST POSEY

warrior with a cruel smile on his lips unhitches his dick from the saddle and jumps down. The leather-wrapped ramrod stands out from his body in a slight arc, turgid and twitching. "How long has this warrior's cock been slapping against the saddle? Who knows? Days? Weeks, even?"

He spots a young shepherd lad trying to hide behind a rock. His big, tough, hard dick twitches up and down in anticipation as he strides over and whacks the lad across the head with his longbow. The youth collapses prone onto the turf. The warrior pulls aside the lad's tunic to reveal a pair of plump brown buns. "This sort of brutality was common in centuries past as mankind struggled to overcome his animal nature."

My cock was rock-hard. I looked up at my reflection in the ceiling mirror. My left hand cradled my nuts while my right hand stroked lightly up and down the throbbing length of my dick. I needed some lubricant. I punched Channel 3: "Lubricants for Masturbation."

A shallow-draft reed coracle bobs lazily on the waters of a blue lake. "This is Lake Texcoco at the time of the Aztec Empire." A young, lithe Aztec fisherman is leaning over the side of the boat. Using a woven sieve, he is scooping up masses of green algae and dumping them into baskets. He passes his hand over his forehead to wipe away the moisture from his eyes. His wiry brown body is glistening with sweat. He is wearing a dirty loincloth fastened about his slender hips. "This Aztec fisherman is gathering spirulina, a protein-rich algae that forms a staple of the diet of the people of Tenochtitlán."

The heat is intense, the burning sun reflecting from the waters of the lake. The young fisherman lies back in the bottom of the boat and closes his eyes. His right hand lazily pulls aside the loincloth and begins to stroke his sturdy brown penis. The sweat drips from his smooth chest and thighs. Soon his cock is swollen from the heat and the stroking. He dips his hand into one of the baskets and removes a generous gob of fresh, cool, slimy spirulina. "Take time now to locate your personal supply of spirulina in your supply locker," the narrator instructs.

148

I jumped up and opened the locker. There it was on the second shelf, a plastic pint-size container labeled SPIRULINA. I pulled off the top as I reclined again. The aroma of fecund life arose from the dank algae within.

The fisherman lazily slathers his hard, brown dick with the green slime. It seems to coat his dick without running down. His hand moves lightly over his entire cock until it is completely coated with the cool, slimy substance. He sighs and lies back, enjoying its coolness against the burning sun.

My own dick was now coated with spirulina, and I began to slide my right hand up and down in a slow, deliberate motion. No need to try to come yet, like Master Bates said. Just enjoy the exquisite sensations produced by this protein-rich slime. Sliding my hand up and down my throbbing cock, I watched the young Aztec on the tube.

"Spirulina slime is one of the most effective lubricants for masturbation." The fisherman's stroking motions become faster and faster, his breathing speeding up as he sucks the hot, moist air of the lake into his lungs. He sighs in pleasure as the slimy spirulina slides across the tender skin of his turgid pole. He groans and arches his hips as gobs of white-hot spunk spray across his chest and belly. He relaxes and smiles. Soon he stands and scoops up handfuls of lake water to wash his sweaty torso. He takes off his loincloth and submerges it in the water, then lays it across the bottom of the boat to dry.

I was close to orgasm, so I stopped jerking. The scene on the tube changed.

Kansas, U.S.A., 1927. A young farmer is on his back under a tractor inside a rough wooden shed. Outside a half-moon shines on an autumn prairie. The man is working on the rear axle of his old tractor. A single kerosene lamp dangles from the rear of the rusty vehicle. His strong, veiny hands are black with grease. His legs protrude from under the tractor, clad in a pair of dirty striped coveralls. He is without a shirt, so his greasy forearms and biceps gleam in the lamplight. The camera moves in on his crotch. A shadow cast by the kerosene lamp outlines the mass of a semierect prick pointing upward and slightly to the right. As the camera moves in tighter on his crotch, a throbbing movement can be detected through the camouflage of the striped fabric. The camera stays in close for about a minute so that we can see the farmer's dick throbbing over and over again through the coveralls. His greasy left hand comes into the frame and begins to massage the swelling lump beneath the cloth.

Medium shot up from between the farmer's legs. He unbuttons his coveralls with his right hand while his left hand continues to rub his prick through the cloth. His right hand works through the fly and pulls out a thick pink-white erection. With another twisting motion he pulls out his swollen nuts and lets them hang down on the crotch seam of the coveralls. He reaches out his left arm to grasp a fat can marked AXLE GREASE. He plunges the fingers of his right hand into the can and scoops up a thick wad of black grease. "Take time now to locate your personal supply of axle grease in your supply locker."

I jumped up and opened the locker. There it was on the second shelf, a plastic pint-size container labeled AXLE GREASE. I pulled off the lid as I reclined again. The aroma of heavy petroleum arose from the blackness within.

I slathered my cock with heavy gobs of the thick black goo while I watched the young farmer with his legs spread apart beneath the tractor. He greases up his white pecker until it shines ebony in the soft light.

Now the farmer starts to beat his meat in earnest. His left hand pulls deftly on his big nuts while his right hand strokes forcefully up and down in a steady rhythm. His blackened greasy dick is like a tractor motor piston moving up and down in the tight cylinder of his right fist. The black grease is too thick to start off. It has to get hot. It has to start smoothing out as your fist and your dick get hotter and hotter.

The young farmer is pushing down with his toes as if he were pushing on the accelerator of his tractor. He's revving the engine while his piston dick moves faster and faster through the hot black grease. You can hear slurping sounds as the axle grease begins to heat up and squish through his fingers. His breath is coming in fast gulps.

He reaches over to the can and lifts out another big wad of grease, smearing it over his stiff ramrod. He needs a lot of lubrication for the heavy pounding he's giving his dick.

The camera moves in for an extreme close-up of the farmer's thick, hard meat. His fist is moving faster and faster. The new grease starts to heat up as it slides around his palm and squishes through his fingers in black gobs. You hear the base of his fist make a thudding sound as it reverberates against his pelvis again and again. He starts to groan, and his butt lifts a couple of inches off the floor of the shed.

Full shot of the farmer's face. The lamplight glistens on the beads of sweat on his forehead. Little bubbles of saliva appear at the corners of his mouth. His jaw clenches with effort.

Close-up of the farmer's crotch from between his knees. His piston dick slides through the black grease faster and faster. He's plowing the fields now. Revving his engine. Going for the big O.

Close-up of his crotch from overhead. "Je-e-ez!" he moans. His back arches. His fist pounds out a heavy beating sound. *Thump! Thump! Thump!* A gasp and a groan and a first spray of thick, fresh cream spurts from his swollen cock. "Je-e-ez!" he groans again as a second creamy ejaculation shoots out and lands on the bib of his coveralls. "O-o-oh!" A third eruption of hot seed leaps into the air and spatters his chest. He slows his fist down and begins to milk his cock. Gushers of white jism flow across his hand and forearm. His arched back relaxes to the floor. His entire frame shivers in the ecstasy of release. His dick is still hard as a rock, coated with streaks of black and white. He breathes deeply as he throws his head back and stretches his legs. The last flows of come seep slowly out of his dick head. "Mmm..." he sighs. "Mmm..."

"Take time now to clean your penis," the narrator instructs.

I wiped the heavy black gunk from my cock with one of the towels. This delaying-orgasm business was leaving my dick raw and swollen. How long could I keep from coming? *The more I delay, the more intense the orgasm will be,* I told myself. I punched the remote control for Channel 8.

The letters on the video screen read, CHANNEL 8—UNENDURABLE PLEASURE INDEFINITELY PROLONGED. My raw dick twitched in anticipation. But wait! Below it were the words PERMISSION TO TAKE THIS COURSE MUST BE OBTAINED FROM THE DIRECTOR OF THE ACADEMY.

I punched Channel 12. After a moment the face of Master Bates appeared on the screen. "Hello!" he said brightly. "How are things going on your first day at KLAMA?"

"Great, just great, Master Bates," I replied. "I've been through several of your course offerings, and they're just wonderful." I paused, wondering if there was going to be a problem with unendurable pleasure indefinitely prolonged.

"Well...?" asked Master Bates.

"I wanted to take the course on Channel 8, but it says I need your permission."

There was a frown on Master Bates's face as he considered my request. He rubbed his chin and scratched his ear in concentration. Finally he replied. "'Unendurable Pleasure Indefinitely Prolonged' is not a course to be taken lightly. It requires nerves of steel and a constitution that is inured to the demands of delayed orgasm. Do you think you can handle it with just one day's experience at the academy?"

I knew that I *had* to experience it. "Please, Master Bates, my time in Kama Loka is limited. I must take this class. Please!" My raw, inflamed prick was throbbing in anticipation. "Please..."

"Very well," he replied, "but I cannot be responsible for the outcome to either your body or your brain. Wait for me in your masturbation module while I gather the special supplies that we will need." The screen went blank.

I lay back on the recliner and flipped through the channels while I waited for Master Bates. I stopped on Channel 4—"Jacking Off in Public Places."

A well-dressed man in his thirties is walking down a crowded city street. He is wearing a dark blue blazer and gray slacks.

"Charlie's fat eight-inch cock needs to be jacked off at least five or six times a day," the narrator begins. "He is masturbating now during a lunch-hour stroll."

Charlie stops to look in the window of a bookstore. Close-up from his waist down through the glass. His right hand is in the pocket of his blazer. "Who would guess that this seemingly innocent, well-dressed gentleman is a heavy jack-off pervert? Notice that his hand movements can hardly be detected. Charlie's philosophy is, Why spend your lunch hour masturbating in some stinky men's room when you can enjoy a great orgasm in the fresh air?"

Flashback: Charlie is getting dressed for work in the morning. He pulls on his trousers. He is not wearing any underwear. Close-up of his pants pocket from the inside. "Notice how Charlie has cleverly cut a long slit on the inside of his right-hand pants pocket." He puts on his shirt and tie. As he puts on his blazer, the camera moves in to a close-up of the blazer pocket. Charlie pulls the jacket pocket open to reveal another slit. He puts his right hand through the slit in the jacket, into his pants pocket, and then through the slit in the trousers to grab his big erect dick. "This is called the double-slit technique. Let's watch it in action in the bookstore."

Charlie enters the bookstore with his seemingly innocent hand in his blazer pocket. He starts to browse along one of the side aisles. He spots a nice-looking young stud in the nonfiction section. "Charlie stops next to the young hunk and decides to have an orgasm while admiring his hot firm ass encased so invitingly in his tight jeans. Charlie's concealed fingers move expertly over the head of his dick—"

There was a sharp knock at the door of the masturbation module. I flipped off the video screen. "Come in!" I called, jumping to my feet.

Master Bates entered, carrying a leather briefcase. He looked at the towel on the floor streaked with green slime and black grease. "I see you've watched our course on lubricants," he said, checking out my cock. "You haven't ejaculated, have you?"

"No, Master Bates, I've been a good boy."

"Excellent. Now, are you sure you want to go through with 'Unendurable Pleasure Indefinitely Prolonged'?"

"Absolutely!"

He spread a fresh, clean towel over the recliner. "Lie down and relax," he instructed. As I lay back, he opened his briefcase and removed several stout leather straps fitted with heavy buckles.

He began by passing a strap around my waist and securing my torso firmly to the lounger. "This procedure requires that you be restrained from any violent motion," he carefully explained. He similarly fastened my wrists, thighs, and ankles. An extra-wide strap was then passed over my chest and shoulders, then under the recliner.

My turgid cock was straining upward toward the ceiling. I looked at my reflection—my slender, naked body circled by black leather straps, my cock red, raw, and twitching. I was definitely ready for unendurable pleasure indefinitely prolonged.

Master Bates held a small bottle of brownish powder, which he began to sprinkle generously over the base of my erect cock, covering my pubic hair and making a wide band around my entire genital area. "Powdered cinnamon," he explained.

"Wha-a-at?" I exclaimed. "Why...?"

He reached into the briefcase and removed a small vial full of something black and shiny. The contents appeared to be quivering! He removed the stopper and began to carefully empty the mysterious substance over the head of my throbbing cock, tapping gently on the bottom of the vial. The head of my dick was soon covered with tiny black moving shapes.

Ants!

Tiny, shiny black ants! Hundreds of them. Within moments they were scurrying all over the head and then the shaft of my tormented tool.

"Voilà!" said Master Bates. "Unendurable pleasure indefinitely prolonged. Of course, this is just the overture. The full effect doesn't begin for at least half an hour. Then you will understand why I warned you.

"For some reason unknown to science," he continued, "ants will not cross a line of cinnamon powder. This means that they will stay confined to the tender tissues of your penis. As they get more frantic, your pleasures will become more unendurable.

"Oh, I almost forgot," he said. He removed a padded leather gag and forced it into my mouth, securing it around the back of my head. "We don't want you to disturb the other students when the going gets tough." He snapped shut his briefcase and turned toward the door. "Enjoy!" he said, giving a little wave. I watched his departure in the overhead mirror.

"*Ummpphh! Ggggf*" I said through the gag.

I was alone with the unendurably pleasurable ants swarming over my rigid dick. Sure enough, they refused to cross the cinnamon dusted around the base of my cock. I looked at one ant in particular. He crawled down the dick shaft and then paused where the pubic hair began. His antennae twitched. He retreated and crawled back up to the head. Dozens of others were making the same maneuver. Up and down, up and down. Circling the tender head. Running around. Crawling. Tickling.

I closed my eyes to concentrate on the sensations emanating from my cock. They were definitely pleasurable but not yet unendurable. Yet I could see that they would very soon become unendurably pleasurable. Hundreds of tiny legs tickled my dick from base to head, sometimes slow, sometimes fast. As the minutes slowly passed, these tiny sensations seemed to amplify until I became aware of each feathery tingle.

As time went by my conscious awareness seemed to be seated not in my head but in the head of my cock. Each small, tingling ant step began to resound like horses' hooves galloping across my swollen genital tissue. The shaft grew rock-hard. I could feel each vein and artery as they engorged to the bursting point with blood. How long had I been in this state? Minutes? Hours? Years? The ants grew frantic. They wanted to return to their nest. They began to make short essays down my urethra. First they probed with their antennae, then they began to increasingly penetrate the dark, moist tube. Now I could feel them crawling several inches inside my throbbing cock meat. More and more of them swarmed toward the dark dick hole. If only I could shoot my load, I could blast them out. I strained upward.

This was truly unendurable. I tried to scream through the gag. *"Ummpphh!"* *Unendurable pleasure. Unendurable pain. Indefinitely prolonged...prolonged...unendurable...*

This *couldn't* go on! I *couldn't* stand it anymore! And yet it *would* go on until my mind snapped.

I must not give in to madness, I told myself. I remembered vaguely somewhere in my pleasure-tormented mind that I could communicate with somebody. Who?

Dr. Wünder! Through the unendurable pleasure I moved my fingers to type HELP! I WANT TO WAKE UP. I WANT TO...

"Wake up! Ted, wake up!" Dr. Wünder was shaking me by my shoulders. "Are you all right?"

I was moaning and shaking. Sweat was running down my face. Dr. Wünder was stroking my head. "Poor boy," he said. "Did your lucid dream get out of control?"

The inside of my shorts was again sticky with expended sperm. I sat up and looked at Dr. Wünder. *"Woo-wee!"* I gasped. I threw my arms around Dr. Wünder's neck. I was so glad to be released from Unendurable Pleasure Indefinitely Prolonged. I kissed him on the cheek.

Dr. Wünder was stroking the back of my neck as he said, "I think that tonight I'd better go with you to Kama Loka and see for myself."

PART FOUR

"Tonight we'll be in Kama Loka together," said Dr. Wünder as he flipped out the divan into a double bed. He pulled shut the heavy drapes of his office windows.

Dr. Wünder handed me the familiar small glass of pink liquid. "Drink your acetylcholine and then lie down and relax, Ted, while I set up the dream monitor."

I downed the acetylcholine and then lay back on one side of the bed as Dr. Wünder placed a firm pillow beneath my head. I caught my last glimpse of the tempting bulge of meat through the crotch of his trousers before Dr. Wünder slipped the lucid-dreaming spectacles over my eyes.

The dream monitor hummed a musical tone as I felt a wave of relaxation sweep over my body. "There won't be any need for the digital gloves tonight since I'll be with you in the lucid state," Dr. Wünder said. "How do you feel?"

"Very relaxed," I replied with a yawn.

"We'll get to the bottom of the mystery of Kama Loka tonight," he said. "I'll be along just as soon as I set up my own frequencies on the dream monitor. Pleasant dreams, Ted. See you in Kama Loka—Dream City of Desire."

A soft tingling at the corners of my eyes signaled the onset of REM sleep, telling me that I was on the threshold of another new adventure. The dream monitor would stabilize my lucidity. Grayish mists shifted and cleared as I looked up. The familiar archway of neon gleamed overhead: WELCOME TO KAMA LOKA.

The man with the leashed dragon was leaning against one of the pylons of the arch. The little dragon was licking his own genitals with a soft slurping sound.

"Good evening, stranger!" the revegen said. "Back again for some more fun?"

"Yes! Er, no! I mean, I'm supposed to meet somebody."

The man with the dragon looked lasciviously at my crotch. "How about me?" he asked. "I'm somebody!" He licked his lips meaningfully.

I looked down at my crotch to see a heavy bulge through the thin trousers. I was wearing a khaki uniform with a thick leather belt and shiny black knee boots. Embroidered shoulder patches showed an insignia of a raised fist above the words GUILT PATROL in gold and black. A shiny gold badge on my chest repeated the raised-fist insignia. At my right side a tooled leather holster held a chrome-plated pistol of bizarre design.

"I'm crazy about men in uniform," the man with the dragon said, rubbing my hardening cock through the cloth of my trousers. "Let's go over there in the bushes." He led me off the road into the gray night mist of Kama Loka.

The bushes were full of rustling sounds. Low voices murmured from all sides.

"Oh, man!" a voice said. "Let me suck that big dick!" Slurping sounds were followed by deep breathing, then gagging. "Please don't choke me with that horse meat!" More gagging ensued, followed by retching sounds. "I can't take any more...please!" Another voice a bit farther away: "Fuck my ass good and hard. That's it! Deeper! Harder! Faster! Meaner!" Groans of agony. "Spread my cheeks with that mule dick! Wider, man, wider!" Sounds of a leather belt hitting soft butt flesh. *"A-a-argh!"*

The man with the dragon fell to his knees in front of me and ran his tongue over the bulge in the coarse fabric of my trousers. "I need to suck some man meat real bad...real bad!" he sighed. I could feel the heat of his breath through the fabric. My cock stiffened, straining upward against the cloth.

The dragon was getting excited. His thorny little dragon dick was twitching, leaking yellow-green secretions. His master tugged down the zipper of my uniform and reached in to feel my throbbing, erect cock.

"Mmm!" he murmured as he extracted my prick from its prison. "Nothing like a big, hard man in uniform." My ramrod stood straight up, glistening in the faint light. It was huge and thick, twice its normal size! But this was Kama Loka—anything could happen. I directed my mental energy toward my throbbing cock and watched it grow and thicken. Shiny drops of precome oozed from the slit. Turgid blue veins pulsed around the shaft.

The revegen slid his hot lips over the engorged cock head. His tongue wrapped around its girth as he licked up the salty secretions. He started to knead my big gonads with both hands as he pushed his lips farther down along the shaft.

"Ummm!" he sighed, breathing in hard when the head of my poker hit the back of his soft palate. His head drove down as he attempted to force my cock into his throat.

All around us the night echoed with harsh sounds of pure lust: "Fuck my skull with that bull dick! Fuck it! Fuck it! *A-a-arrgghh!*"

I grabbed the back of my cocksucker's head and pulled it down onto my pile-driver dick. It began slowly to force its way deeper into his hot, slimy throat. I wanted it all the way down until he gagged on its length.

A flashing red light pierced the gloom. I heard the screech of brakes and the squeal of tires.

The bushes suddenly resounded with a hubbub of voices and the thuds of running feet: "It's the Guilt Patrol!" someone cried. "It's the chief of the Guilt Patrol! Run!" A bolt of blue lightning streaked through the bushes and hit the man with the dragon in the middle of his shoulders. His mouth slid off my cock as he tumbled backward and hit the ground. The little dragon ran off into the mist, screeching.

A bulky figure loomed out of the mist: tall and muscular, with the same khaki uniform that I was wearing. In his right hand he held the same bizarre chrome-plated pistol, a whiff of blue smoke curling up from the barrel. His badge read CHIEF. A long, thick cock hung down his right leg, bulging through the cloth

I studied his face through the mist. "Dr. Wünder!" I shouted, finally recognizing the features.

He looked me over impassively. "What's that?"

"Dr. Wünder?" I asked. It certainly looked like Dr. Wünder, but I was no longer sure.

"Don't know what you're talking about," he answered. "You must be the new recruit. Good job trapping that Rebel. That's the last we'll see of him."

We looked down at the still figure of the man who had been sucking my cock. He was rapidly dissolving into a blue vapor, the little dragon nowhere to be seen.

"Come on, let's get back to headquarters." The chief grabbed me by the arm and pulled me toward a shiny black patrol car. "Get in!" he commanded. "I have some questions to ask you when we get back."

The tires screeched as we careened off into the night. Our flashing red light carved strange shapes in the mist.

"Uh…Chief," I asked, "what was his actual offense—I mean, the man you shot?"

"Shot? Oh, you mean the Rebel I just zapped? Where have you been? He's one of the Shameless Rebels who don't feel any guilt—that's why he had to be zapped with a lethal guilt bolt. Didn't you take the Oath of Shame when you joined the Guilt Patrol?"

The chief looked at me strangely as he applied the brakes and stopped in front of a massive concrete bunkerlike structure. Engraved in the concrete were the words GUILT PATROL HEADQUARTERS.

As we entered, two armed guards with the same khaki uniforms saluted the chief. "Good evening, Chief Kokk!" they said in unison, stopping and standing at attention.

He nodded to the guards, then led me down a long, dim concrete corridor. At the very end of the hall was a door with a plaque reading CHIEF KOKK. The chief sat behind a massive stainless steel desk and motioned me to sit on a low stool in the middle of the room. He eyed me suspiciously.

The metal stool was cold through the cloth of my khaki uniform, and a chill went up my spine as I stared into the chief's dark, suspicious eyes.

"What were you doing in the bushes with that Rebel?" he asked me.

"Uhh…we were just talking, Chief," I replied lamely.

"Just talking, huh? You sure he wasn't sucking your cock? That Shameless Rebel was a notorious cocksucker." Chief Kokk scowled ferociously. "And he didn't feel any guilt about his unnatural practices!"

I swallowed hard. My mouth was dry. What was the punishment for feeling no guilt? Elimination? Torture?

"Don't you have anything to say?" The chief stood up behind the massive desk. I could see the shape of his big dick hanging down the right leg of his uniform. He saw my eyes staring at his crotch. With a faint smile he lightly rubbed his cock through the cloth. It started to stiffen.

"Stand up and unzip your pants," he commanded.

He watched impassively as I pulled down the zipper of my khaki uniform.

"Now pull out your dick."

My shame was overcome by my fear of the chief as I let my nerdy little cock hang out. He looked down at it with contempt.

"Not very big, is it?" he said.

"No, Chief Kokk."

"Nobody is supposed to be admitted to the Guilt Patrol with a small dick. We require at least nine inches of heavy meat and testicles at least as big as jumbo Grade A hen's eggs. How did you get that uniform?"

"I…I…I just found it on me an hour ago."

"Take out your nuts."

I reached into my trousers and let my testicles hang out over the bottom of my fly. Chief Kokk smiled as he appraised them.

"Not any bigger than a couple of grapes. Not big enough for a Guilt Patrol recruit. You're a complete phony. Where did you come from?"

Chief Kokk continued to massage his thick tool through the leg of his uniform trousers. Long and massive, it reached down almost to his knee, its stiffening length held down by the tightly stretched cloth. I couldn't help staring with desire and fascination at its huge bulk.

"Are you a spy?" he demanded. A faint wet spot appeared at the head of his cock and started to spread through the fabric of his trouser leg. His excitement increased as he barked, "You're an impostor! Take off that uniform! *Now!*"

I quickly pulled off my uniform and boots and let them fall in a pile on the concrete floor. The chief took his right hand away from his big hard dick and removed from his belt a heavy two-foot-long billy club. He unexpectedly smashed it full force against my stomach. I doubled over in agony.

"Get the underwear and socks off too!" he barked.

I straightened up despite the pain and managed to pull off the rest of my clothing.

"Stand up straight!" ordered the chief. I stood at attention. He looked at my naked body with a sneer. "Your cock ain't worth shit," he said. He brought the billy club down hard against my groin. *Thwack!* And again: *Thwack!*

Searing pains shot through my loins. "Please, Chief Kokk!" I moaned.

"Fold up those clothes and put them in the corner of the room away from the door," he ordered. I quickly followed his instructions, making a neat stack of the folded uniform. I placed the boots beside the pile.

"Now get over here and sit!" He tapped the metal stool with the end of the billy club.

I shivered as my naked butt pressed against the cold metal. My balls hung down over the front edge of the seat. I looked down. My cock was getting hard, starting to stand straight up.

Chief Kokk rubbed the end of the billy club against the underside of my dick. "Some guys like their genitals worked over. You must be one of them." A cruel smile played across his mouth. He smashed the club across my erect cock, once from the right and then from the left. I covered it with my hands.

"Please, Chief, don't hurt me," I begged. "Please!"

"Put your hands behind your back!" he commanded. I felt the bite of metal against my skin as he handcuffed my wrists. "That's what I like to see," he said. "A Shameless Rebel ready to take his punishment like a man." He rubbed his own huge dick through his trouser leg. The wet stain on the cloth was spreading, getting darker as his excitement increased.

"Tell me who sent you!" he snapped, his voice rising almost to a shout as he mercilessly clubbed my helpless cock. *Thwack! Thwack! Thwack! Thwack!* My defenseless dick seemed to be getting harder and bigger as it absorbed the kinetic energy of the billy club. Sharp white flashbulbs exploded on my retinas with each heavy blow. *Thwack! Thwack!*

The chief paused, then began tapping the billy club lightly against my totally vulnerable balls, pressing them against the rim of the stool. Chief Kokk ran his tongue around his lips as he began to tap my testicles harder. "Tell me who sent you, or I'm going to smash your little balls like grapes."

I moaned in pain. I probably had to tell the truth, but the truth was that I really *was* a spy. I had come to Kama Loka to get information for Dr. Wünder. Chief Kokk's club pounded against my nuts with increasing force. *Thunk! Thunk!*

I couldn't take it anymore. "Please stop smashing my balls!" I implored. "I'll tell! Dr. Wünder sent me...I was supposed to meet him tonight in Kama Loka."

The chief halted his painful ministrations with the billy club in mid stroke. His eyes narrowed. "Where does this Dr. Wünder come from?" he asked.

I gulped. How to explain? "He's from Saratoga University."

"Never heard of Saratoga University," he said. "What does this Dr. Wünder look like?"

"He looks...like you... I...I mean, y-you look...like him," I stammered.

"Bullshit!" shouted the chief. I winced as he banged the billy club against the metal rim of the stool, right next to my throbbing, bruised gonads. "What are you guilty of?" he demanded.

"It's not my fault," I gasped. "I never meant any harm."

"That's not what the record shows," he shot back. "I have some testimonies you ought to hear." He pulled a small cassette recorder out of a desk drawer and pushed the PLAY button. A crackle of static was followed by a taped voice. I recognized Bruce, the waiter at the Aphrodisia Café.

"That's right," Bruce was saying. "He came in here and scarfed down a special of the evening—a big, thick, long, juicy buffalo penis—and a bottle of very expensive French wine. Then he refused to pay the bill and didn't leave a tip and disappeared into the night."

"That's not true!" I protested, shifting my ass on the cold stool. "He tore up the check."

"Likely story!" said the chief. "Listen to this one and see if you can deny your guilt."

This time it was Blond Angel, whom I had encountered on my first night in Kama Loka: "He forced me to jerk him off, and then he made me suck his colossal dick, and then he tried to gag and choke me with it, and then he nearly drowned me with two big hot loads of love juice down my throat and in my face and all over my chest and forearms. I'll never forget it."

"That's not true!" I yelled. "He wanted to do it! He had written on his back WILL WORK FOR SEX. He begged me for it!"

"You're guilty as hell, you nerdy pervert!" growled Chief Kokk. He started to tap the shaft of my cock with the billy club. "Listen to this one, and let's see what kind of flimsy apology you can come up with." A strange and painful sexual excitement began to build up in my swollen nuts as they lay against the cold metal of the stool. My cock thudded against my stomach with each tap of the chief's club.

A burst of static, and then a new witness. I immediately recognized the voice of Dr. Hung Soo Fat.

"I give leally nice big, long, thick plick!" Dr. Hung's voice was saying. "I give led head and blue veins, fill up nuts nice and full with Locky Load love juice. He lefuse to pay full amount as agleed."

"That's a lie!" I screamed, straining against my handcuffs. "He gave me a discount!"

"*You're* the liar!" Chief Kokk shouted in my face. He clubbed my dick back and forth from left to right with the full force of his muscular forearm. An unrecognizable sound tore from my throat. Dribbles of slime began to emerge from my dick hole. My cock and balls seemed to be swelling up bigger and bigger with each blow of the club. My excitement was increasing.

The next witness's voice that came crackling from the tape recorder was that of Master Bates, director of the Kama Loka Academy of Masturbatory Arts.

"He disappeared in the middle of our class on 'Unendurable Pleasure Indefinitely Prolonged,'" he was saying. "The extra tuition for that special course is still outstanding. Also, he didn't clean up his room."

"You better start admitting guilt, you faggy twerp," Chief Kokk threatened. "Let's get the Guilt Meter running." He placed a metal headband around my temples. Thin wires ran to a large dial on the wall, numbered clockwise from 0 to 100. The needle swayed around 5.

"We've got to get that guilt level up, boy," snarled the chief. "Listen to this, and then we'll see what you have to say."

The voice of Chico of Colón moaned from the tape. "*Ay, madrecita!* That fucker came in the Rectum Rodeo and used his Megameat to tear up my anus and rearrange my guts! He pounded my ass to hell, man! Then he filled me up with his hot and sticky white love juice until it came out of my mouth. I have to cancel my act for three weeks to recover from that night! *Te amo,* Megameat!"

The needle of the Guilt Meter started to climb as I listened to Chico's testimony. Everything he said was absolutely true. I had used his helpless asshole for my selfish pleasure. The needle climbed to 20.

"You better start absorbing guilt real fast," the chief said, putting the sole of his boot on my inflamed nuts and crushing them against the rim of the stool. "What else are you guilty of?" His rigid cock meat throbbed through his trousers just inches away from my eyes. "What else!"

My nuts were turning to paste. "I'm guilty for having tiny little testicles!" I gasped. The Guilt Meter shot up to 30.

"What else?" He grabbed my hair and pulled my face against the right leg of his khaki uniform. I could feel the throbbing of his huge horse dick beneath the cloth.

"I'm guilty for having a little tiny nerdy dick," I choked. "I need to have the big dick of a real man shoved down my throat until I smother in cock meat and drown in spunk!"

The Guilt Meter shot up to 50. My bruised and throbbing cock twitched in preorgasmic jerks. Clear sap oozed from the urethra. Chief Kokk stepped back and removed the chrome-plated pistol from his holster. "You ain't never gonna get your slimy Rebel mouth on *my* cock," he said, sneering. He took aim at my crotch with his guilt gun. "Let's see how much guilt you can absorb, pussy boy!" He pulled the trigger.

An icy-hot blue bolt of guilt slammed into the base of my cock. *Zap!* The Guilt Meter jumped, then fell again to 50.

"It ain't enough to feel the pain, boy," Chief Kokk grunted. "You've got to absorb it." He aimed at my bruised nuts and pulled the trigger once more.

Zap! Zap! The Guilt Meter climbed and steadied at 55. I realized that when the needle reached 100, I would finally shoot my rocks off—but was it an orgasm I could survive? A thin whiff of blue vapor rose from my scorched testicles.

"I'm guilty of being a spy for the Shameless Rebels!" I gasped. "I came to get information about the power structure of Kama Loka." I saw the Guilt Meter climb to 60.

Chief Kokk's lips widened into a twisted, sadistic smile as he took aim at the head of my throbbing dick. *Zap! Zap! Zap!* My cock slammed against my stomach in recoil from the blue guilt bolt. The needle climbed to 68 and steadied. Chief Kokk's sexual excitement was all too obvious as he kneaded his big, thick erection. *"What else!"* he demanded.

"I'm guilty of sucking men's dicks through the glory holes at Susie's Suck Stop!" The needle climbed to 75. "A couple of nights ago, I sucked off six different big-dicked dudes and lapped up the spilled jism off the plywood door of the toilet stall." The needle climbed to 80. "I had to be chained like an animal to the toilet pipes. That's all I am! A cock-hungry slave animal!" The needle climbed to 85.

"That guilt level has to get up to 100!" The chief screamed, breathing heavily as he took aim again at my crotch.

Zap! Zap! Zap! Zap! Four stinging bolts of guilt plowed into my cock shaft. The Guilt Meter jumped to 90.

"I'm a shameless, cocksucking, little-dicked Rebel spy!" I screamed. More wispy blue vapor rose from my burning dick. The chief slugged me twice across the face with the barrel of his guilt gun, right and left. I felt my jaw crack as the Guilt Meter climbed to 95.

I had to make it to 100. I had to shoot my load. What else was I guilty of?

"*What else!*" shouted Chief Kokk as he aimed at my crotch point-blank.

"My ass has never been fucked!" I screamed. The needle jumped to 98. Chief Kokk cocked the trigger of his guilt gun.

"*I need a big dick to split my ass open!*" I sobbed as the point-blank guilt bolt blasted my dick one final time. The Guilt Needle hit 100. The stool fell over, and my back hit the concrete floor as my tortured cock spewed geysers of hot man cream all over my stomach, chest, and face. I saw visions of flashing blue explosions going off in my head, and then I blacked out.

When my awareness returned, I saw that Chief Kokk's strong arms had lifted me off the floor and set me upright on the stool.

"Looks like you took as much guilt as you could stand, boy!" he said. The Guilt Meter stood quivering at 50. My trembling body was covered with sweat and sperm. The chief slapped my face hard on both sides. I felt a trickle of blood run down the corner of my mouth.

"What's that you said, boy?" he demanded.

"When?" I asked weakly.

The chief smashed my nuts with the billy club. "What's that you screamed when the Guilt Meter hit 100?" he asked once more, smacking my nuts again, harder this time.

"I said I needed a big dick," I answered timidly.

Chief Kokk pressed the tip of his club against my right nut and began to crush it against the metal stool. "What else did you say?" He pressed harder. I screamed in agony.

"I said I needed a big dick to...to...to split my ass open," I sobbed.

"That's what I thought you said, and I always give Rebels what they deserve to get." He opened a closet door and dragged out a hideous device. I stared at it in sick fascination.

"Meet the Iron Duke!" said the chief. He patted the shiny steel cone that rose from a sturdy metal platform. "Come on over here and get acquainted."

I staggered to my feet and shuffled over to where the Iron Duke stood, erect and menacing. The chief ran his palm over the cold steel. "Twenty-two *tall* inches of steel death," he mused. "One inch in diameter at the top, eight inches in diameter at the bottom. We don't want to split your ass open all at once—just gradually as you slide down the length of the Iron Duke. Let's get started!"

The chief grabbed my shoulders and stood me over the horrible device. My arms strained behind my back against the shackles of my handcuffs, but I was too weak to resist. As the chief pushed me down, my knees began to buckle, and I felt the cold, hard tip of the Iron Duke enter my anus.

"Please, Chief," I gasped weakly, "I've told you all I know. I'm guilty as hell."

A crooked smile curled his lips. "You asked for it, Rebel! You said you wanted your ass split open." He pushed down hard on my shoulders. I felt the Iron Duke plow deeper into my rectum. My anus spread apart painfully. The hard, implacable steel cone of the Iron Duke was about three inches into my asshole.

Chief Kokk stood back and looked with satisfaction at his helpless prisoner impaled on the Iron Duke. "Your own body weight will gradually split your ass open," he said. "Your bent knees will get increasingly tired and weak as gravity pulls you down." He sat on the edge of his desk and began to unzip his uniform trousers.

"I'm just going to sit here and beat my meat while I watch the termination of another Shameless Rebel," he said, reaching into his fly and with some difficulty unleashing his huge, thick, hard cock. He hauled out his heavy balls and let them dangle over the edge of the desk. He began to slap the naked underside of his erect dick with the billy club.

My knees were indeed getting weaker, and I began to inch downward on the terrible, lethal cone of the Iron Duke. My rectum burned with unbearable agony. Low animal groans escaped my throat.

Chief Kokk's thick, beefy dick bounced against his shirtfront as he slammed it with the billy club. "This is how a real man beats his meat!" he breathed. Shiny threads of precome trailed down his massive shaft. "I like to shoot my wad when I see a Rebel asshole split open, when the flesh starts to tear and the blood starts to spurt!"

My knees began to give way completely. The cold shaft of the Iron Duke slid several inches deeper into my distended ass tube.

"Any second now," moaned the chief. "I want to see that flesh rip open. I want to see a lot of blood!" He grabbed the thick shaft of his big cock in his fist and started pounding it up and down. His breath heaved out in gasps.

I slid farther down the Iron Duke. I could feel the tissues of my rectum start to tear open. Blood and mucus began to run down the shaft of the monstrous torture device.

"Please!" I screamed. "You're splitting me open!" The pain was unbelievably excruciating. *"You're splitting me open!"*

"Take it easy, Ted. Relax. You can take it."

It was Dr. Wünder's voice. "Just relax," he whispered, "and let me do the work." I was lying on my stomach on the divan in his office. The heavy weight of his big frame was pressing me to the mattress. His thick fuck tool was entering my virgin rectum, stretching it out, plowing deeper. He kissed my ear and whispered, "I won't split you open, Ted. I just want to stretch that tight, hot little virgin ass. I want to take you to *unendurable pleasure indefinitely prolonged.*"

"How do you know about that?" I asked. "You weren't in Kama Loka that night, were you?"

"Yes, I was, Ted," Dr. Wünder replied. "I was there every night. I was all the authority figures in your dreams. I was the referee at the Rectum Rodeo. I was the Sukmaster and Jenkins. I was Dr. Hung. I was Master Bates. I was Chief Kokk. Now I'm the Iron Duke, plowing into your guts."

"But...why?" I sobbed with relief. "Why didn't you tell me?"

Dr. Wünder pushed his thick, meaty ramrod deeper into my asshole. "I knew you needed a man fuck real bad, but first you needed to get rid of your guilt. You're actually the first real success with my new Lucid Dream Therapy. Your reward will be unendurable pleasure indefinitely prolonged."

"Dr. Wünder, *te amo!*" I sighed. The throbbing shaft of his huge prick plowed deeper into my guts.

"You don't feel guilty, do you, Ted?"

"No!" I gasped. "No! Fuck me hard...and slow...and long!"

He plowed my fuck hole deeper. It was unendurable pleasure, and it was... *indefinitely prolonged.*

Other books of interest from
ALYSON PUBLICATIONS

☐ **B-BOY BLUES,** by James Earl Hardy. A seriously sexy, fiercely funny black-on-black love story. A walk on the wild side turns into more than Mitchell Crawford ever expected. An Alyson best-seller you shouldn't miss.

☐ **BECOMING VISIBLE,** edited by Kevin Jennings. The *Lambda Book Report* states that "*Becoming Visible* is a groundbreaking text and a fascinating read. This book will challenge teens and teachers who think contemporary sex and gender roles are 'natural' and help break down the walls of isolation surrounding lesbian, gay, and bisexual youth."

☐ **CODY,** by Keith Hale. Trottingham Taylor, "Trotsky" to his friends, is new to Little Rock. Washington Damon Cody has lived there all his life. Yet when they meet, there's a familiarity, a sense that they've known each other before. Their friendship grows and develops a rare intensity, although one is gay and the other is straight.

☐ **THE GAY FIRESIDE COMPANION,** by Leigh W. Rutledge. "Rutledge, 'The Gay Trivia Queen,' has compiled a myriad gay facts in an easy-to-read volume. This book offers up the offbeat, trivial, and fascinating from the history and life of gays in America." —Buzz Bryan in *Lambda Book Report*

☐ **MY BIGGEST O,** edited by Jack Hart. What was the best sex you ever had? Jack Hart asked that question of hundreds of gay men and got some fascinating answers. Here are summaries of the most intriguing of them. Together they provide an engaging picture of the sexual tastes of gay men.

☐ **MY FIRST TIME,** edited by Jack Hart. Hart has compiled a fascinating collection of true stories by men across the country, describing their first same-sex encounters. *My First Time* is an intriguing look at just how gay men begin the process of exploring their sexuality.

☐ **THE PRESIDENT'S SON,** by Krandall Kraus. "President Marshall's son is gay. The president, who is beginning a tough battle for reelection, knows it but can't handle it. *The President's Son* is a delicious, oh-so-thinly-veiled tale of a political empire gone insane. A great read." —Marvin Shaw in *The Advocate*

☐ **TWO TEENAGERS IN 20: WRITINGS BY GAY AND LESBIAN YOUTH,** edited by Ann Heron. "Designed to inform and support teenagers dealing on their own with minority sexual identification. The thoughtful, readable accounts focus on feelings about being homosexual, reactions of friends and families, and first encounters with other gay people." —*School Library Journal*

a